SAINT JOAN: THE GIRL SOLDIER

SAINT JOAN

THE GIRL SOLDIER

By Louis de Wohl

ILLUSTRATED BY HARRY BARTON

IGNATIUS PRESS   SAN FRANCISCO

© 1957 by Louis de Wohl

First edition published by Farrar, Straus and Cudahy, Inc.
Published with ecclesiastical approval

Cover art by Christopher J. Pelicano
Cover design by Riz Boncan Marsella

Published in 2001 by Ignatius Press, San Francisco
All rights reserved
ISBN 978-0-89870-822-6
Library of Congress control number 2001088861
Printed in the United States of America ∞
Manufactured by Thomson-Shore, Dexter, MI (USA); RMA589LS619, April, 2013

CONTENTS

Author's Note

The lives of saints are history, for saints make history, and, what is more, they make it the way God likes it best. History without the saints is all warfare, battles, countries enslaved or freed, actions of rulers, change of power from one country to another. But from time to time God points toward the way he wants things done, and the pointer he uses is time and again a saint.

Saints are people, and they are not always peaceful people. They can fight, and indeed they must fight whenever they come across evil. This, then, is the story of a great fighter of God who was a saint. And this fighter, this saint, was a girl. She made history in leading her poor, oppressed country to victory. She made history also by showing by her wonderful example that the very first thing we need if we want to win through is faith.

In the course of my life I have read a great many books about her, and every one of them has taught me a little more about her. Today I no longer remember the names of all the authors, but I am grateful to every one of them.

You too will one day have forgotten the name of this author. But I don't think you will ever forget the saint about whom I have written: lovely, glorious, young Joan of Arc.

I

VOICES BECKON

"MAY I GO, FATHER?"

Farmer d'Arc gave his daughter Joan a long, searching
look. Why was she so different from his other children—
poor little Catherine who was dead now, God rest her
soul, and the two boys, fine boys, both of them? Not
that Joan wasn't a good girl. She was obedient enough,
she did her work well, and she was devout. Good Father
Minet said so again and again. But one never knew what
she was thinking.

Farmer d'Arc looked at his wife. Isabelle was sitting in her old armchair, stitching away at a linen shirt. She did not look up and she said nothing, but then she wouldn't. She knew it was up to him to make the decision.

There was nothing to it, really. Joan wanted to go to visit her cousin Durand Laxart, at nearby Petit Burey, for a week. Nothing to it at all, and yet there was something going on in that firm little head of hers.

Farmer d'Arc gave a sigh. He had dreamed about Joan recently, several times, and always it was the same dream: she was going to run away with soldiers.

Joan looked straight into his eyes. "I'm doing nothing bad, Father."

She must have guessed his thoughts, but her words were a relief. She never lied; he knew that.

"Very well, then. You may go."

"Thank you, Father." She gave him one of her quick, gentle kisses, walked over to her mother and embraced her.

Isabelle took her daughter's face into her hands. "Come back to us", she said softly. "Come back safe and sound, my Joan." Reluctantly her hands went back to her work.

Joan smiled at her and walked away without a further word.

Farmer d'Arc went to the door. He could see her cross the garden. She was carrying a small bundle. "Must have picked it up on the bench outside", he thought. "She knew I was going to give her permission to go."

She was walking on briskly, her simple red dress billowing in the wind; topped by her long, black hair, it made her look like a little pillar of fire and smoke moving across the ground.

The bell of the village church began to clang.

Farmer d'Arc crossed himself and prayed. So did Isabelle inside and all the villagers of Domrémy. So did the villagers of all other places in Lorraine, and in Burgundy and in France and in all other Christian countries, the people in the cities and towns, bishops and noblemen and simple folks, all made one by their Faith.

The little pillar of fire and smoke stopped too for a minute and then moved on.

Farmer d'Arc stepped back into the room. "It's only for a week or two", he said. "And he's a reliable enough fellow, is Durand Laxart. He can do with a pair of hands, too, just now. And yet, I wish I hadn't given her permission. . . ."

"You couldn't stop her", Isabelle said quietly.

He frowned. "She's only seventeen, and I'm her father."

"Oh, I don't mean *that*, Jacques."

"Well, what do you mean, then?" He was a little angry now, and he would have liked to raise his voice, but he did not. Isabelle was not an ordinary woman. She had been on pilgrimage to Rome in her time, all the way there and back on foot, of course. It was a journey almost as dangerous as a voyage to the Holy Land itself, with highway robbers and with half a hundred little wars being waged between some feudal lords or local knights, and having to beg for food and shelter many a time. She had made it and even seen the Pope himself and many of the cardinals, and she had come back safely. "Isabelle Romée" they called her now, "Isabelle-who-has-been-to-Rome". It was like a badge of distinction granted for great courage and devotion, and he was proud of her. He would not raise his voice to her, not to Isabelle Romée.

She was staring into the flames of the log fire in the fireplace.

"There's something about her", she said in a low voice. "Have you ever looked at her when she's praying? Strange she looks, as if there be no life in her. Like her sister looked—on her deathbed. I touched her arm once; she didn't feel it."

"Giving herself airs. Many young girls do", he growled.

Isabelle shook her head. "Not she. And you ought to know her better than that, too."

"I don't know her", he said wearily. "That's just it. I can't make her out. Sometimes, sometimes I wonder how it is that you and I can have a child like her."

Isabelle nodded. "It hasn't always been like that, has it? Only these last few years. As if something had happened to her. I asked her about it, too, but she wouldn't talk, not even to me." She was bending her head over her work again. "I wonder . . ." she said.

"What about?" he asked in an uneasy voice.

"I wonder whether she is going to come back to us."

"What?"

Isabelle looked up. There were tears in her eyes. "I told you you couldn't stop her", she said. "Neither could I—or anybody. She's going because she must go."

"Has she told you . . . ?"

"Not a word. I just feel it. She must go. I'm not even sure whether she *likes* it. It's like . . . like obeying."

"Obeying whom?"

"God", Isabelle said.

Durand Laxart was sitting in front of his little house when he saw her coming. His eyes lit up and he grinned cheerfully. He liked his little cousin, but his face fell when, after the first handshake, she told him: "Get your hat and stick, Durand dear. We must go."

"G–g–go? Where to?"

"To Vaucouleurs, of course, silly."

Durand Laxart took a deep breath. "Joan, you know as well as I do what happened when we went there last time. I did exactly what you told me to do, and what was the result?"

She threw her head back, laughing. "You met Captain Robert de Baudricourt just as I told you you would, didn't you?"

"Yes, but he didn't believe a word of what I said. And he told me to take you back to your father and let him give you a good hiding."

She was still laughing. "But you didn't tell him, and nobody gave me a hiding."

"He also told me", Durand went on, "to tell your father to go marry you off to somebody. I didn't do that either, I know, but I'm not so sure I shouldn't have."

"I shall never marry", Joan said, suddenly very serious. "I vowed I wouldn't, so I won't. But I must go to Vaucouleurs."

Durand, a sturdy man in his early thirties, with a nice, open face and apple cheeks, raised his hands in protest. "What can I do to make you give up that idea, Joan? We are simple people. We can't talk to nobles and the likes of them. They just laugh at us when we do."

"What does it matter if they laugh, as long as they do what I tell them?" Joan said. "And they will, you know. I wasn't a bit disappointed when you didn't succeed last time, was I, Cousin Durand?"

"N-no, but . . ."

"And I wasn't, because I knew beforehand that you wouldn't succeed. My Voices told me you wouldn't."

"They did? Then why . . . ?"

"They told me to go all the same. You did deliver the message I gave you then, didn't you?"

"Yes, I did, but . . ."

"What did you say? Repeat it for me, will you?"

Durand gave a shrug. "I said to Captain de Baudricourt, 'Sir Captain,' I said, 'young Joan d'Arc is waiting outside, the daughter of Jacques d'Arc and Isabelle Romée from Domrémy, and she's my cousin, though I'm sixteen years older than she is, and she has asked me to ask you to give her a horse and armor and some men to go with her so that she . . . so that she . . .' "

"All right, go on, go on!"

" 'So that she can go to see the gentle dauphin and save France for him' ", Durand went on. "I said it to him. It's crazy enough, but I said it."

"You forgot something, didn't you?" Joan asked. "The bit about Orléans?"

"Ah, yes, I forgot that. That is, I forgot it now, but I did tell him then: 'My cousin Joan says she is sent by God to save Orléans from the English.' And Captain de Baudricourt laughed at that and said, 'There, you can see that it's all nonsense about that cousin of yours. Orléans needn't be saved by anybody. It's a French city still and no Englishman anywhere near it.' And he called me all sorts of names in the manner such gentlemen have when they're angry and speaking to one like me."

"Quite", Joan said softly. "Quite. But now Orléans is besieged by the English, isn't it?"

Durand stared at her, wide-eyed. "So it is, by the saints", he said. "Why, I never thought of that. So it is. H-how did you know that at the time? No, don't tell me. Your Voices again . . ."

Joan asked, still very softly: "Don't you believe in my Voices?"

The young farmer scratched his head. "Tell you the truth, Cousin Joan, I don't know what to believe. There is a saying, I know, about a woman who would save France, when another woman had brought France down. . . ."

"I don't care about any such sayings. But I'm under orders to go and see the gentle dauphin and save France for him, and the first thing I am told to do is to go to Vaucouleurs and see Captain Robert de Baudricourt. So I'm going to do that, whether you're coming with me or not."

"You can't go alone", he said, horrified. "A young girl going alone across the country in times like these!"

"Very well, then, come with me."

An idea came to Durand. "Did you tell your parents where you're going?" he asked innocently.

"No, they only know I'm going to see you."

"Ah." The young farmer tried to give his voice the ring of authority. "Surely your Voices can't ask you to break the fourth commandment—to honor father and mother? If they did, how could they be *good* voices?" He was breathing heavily after his effort.

"My Voices said nothing to me about telling my parents", Joan said simply. "It was I who decided not to tell them because they might not have wanted to let me go. But as it is God who has asked me to go, I would go even if I had a hundred fathers and a hundred mothers. I didn't tell them because I didn't want to hurt them."

"You have an answer to everything", Durand said dully. But another answer came to his mind, the answer given by a certain young Boy twelve years of age, to his parents: "Did you not know that I must be about my Father's business?" He shivered a little. Joan was right. If it was God who ordered her to do what she did, God had to be obeyed first. Could he, Durand, afford to say no to Joan?

He had many good reasons why he should not go. His wife was not well. He had work to do. The journey was not without danger. But from his innermost heart he knew that his real reason was that he did not wish to be laughed at again by the haughty captain in Vaucouleurs. That's what it was, and Joan was looking at him all the time, reading his thoughts the way the good priest in church read his missal.

He smiled ruefully. "I'm coming with you."

"Good", Joan said. "And you needn't worry. This time I'm going to do the talking myself."

2

PERMISSION DENIED

NOT AGAIN", said Captain Robert de Baudricourt, when Bertrand de Poulengy came to announce that the young yokel from Petit Burey was back, together with his cousin from Domrémy.

The captain was sitting in his favorite room, the round tower room, where he used to have his council of war not so very long before, when his castle was under siege. From here he had a magnificent view downhill. He could see the entire town and the silver ribbon that was the river Meuse. There was no need for any war councils now, not because there was no more war—there was—but because the war was now being fought in a few other parts of the unfortunate country.

Robert de Baudricourt was a florid man in his late forties, no better and no worse than most military men of his time. He had a knack of twisting his short, brown beard when he was puzzled about something, and he was puzzled now. "Why, I chased the young idiot away six or eight months ago, when he first came with that wretched girl-cousin of his, didn't I?"

"You did, sir captain", said Bertrand de Poulengy.

"And I told him to take her back to her father and let him give her a good thrashing. It doesn't seem to have helped much. What is it he wants now?"

"He wants you to hear what the girl has to say", Bertrand said calmly.

"Oh, he does, does he? As if I hadn't got anything else to do than to listen to her babblings! There are half a dozen people outside who want an audience with me—good and respected citizens of the town, some of them. Why in the name of thunder should I waste my time on some chit of a girl? Tell 'em to go away before I have 'em both frog-marched down the hill." He had talked himself into a rage. "Thunder and lightning, what's this miserable country coming to you that we should have to listen to such people?"

"We don't seem to be doing so very well on our own, if I may say so", young Bertrand said drily.

Robert de Baudricourt's eyes narrowed. "You are a good officer and you come from a good family," he drawled, "but even you must remember that you're talking to your superior."

The young man gave him a stiff little bow, and the grim captain relented. "I don't say you're not right", he growled. "It seems to be our destiny to live in a time when we are always beaten—beaten by the Burgundians, beaten by the English. It's a crying shame, Bertrand, it really is. The flower of French knighthood, men with a string of noble ancestors going back hundreds of years—and beaten by English archers, vulgar backwoodsmen . . ."

"But strong fellows", young Bertrand said. "About that girl . . ."

"Strong, strong—they don't stick to the rules, that's what it is", Robert de Baudricourt bellowed. "They don't fight in a knightly manner. What's the good of our wearing all that heavy armor if they pierce it with their confounded crossbows? That weapon should be forbidden, that's what I always say. Archers, pah."

"About that girl, sir . . ."

"And they beat us every time. But it's not only their doing. What matters in war is leadership, my boy, leadership. And who's leading us? Men without a shred of confidence in what they're doing. And why don't they have any confidence? Because the man they're fighting for has none himself. Charles the Dauphin—he'd be King Charles the Seventh if he were crowned. Seven—

that's an unlucky number, surely. It must be, when I think of our poor, dear, dilly-dallying, penniless good-for-nothing of a dauphin for whom I have the honor of guarding the good fortress of Vaucouleurs. There, now go and report to the dauphin's court what I called him."

"I'm not an informer, sir", Bertrand de Poulengy said stiffly.

The captain grinned at him. "Of course you're not, my dear boy. But even if you were, it wouldn't have the slightest effect. The great nobles all around the poor dauphin are telling him worse things and calling him worse names to his face every day. And what does he do? He just smiles and occasionally says something nice and pointed. He can't afford to hit back, really to hit back. He needs them too much. He's got to borrow money from them. He hasn't got fifty francs in his royal pocket, or so they tell me."

"But surely, sir, there is the money coming in from taxation."

"Taxation! Half of it, three-quarters of it, never reaches the royal treasury. Too many middlemen, my boy—middlemen with sticky hands. The gold just sticks to their hands, if you see what I mean. Ah, it's all hopeless. And in the meantime the English are masters of half of France, and now they'll get Orléans—you'll see they will—and then the dauphin can go and flee south, still farther south, with no army between him and the enemy. Poor France." The captain poured himself a goblet of wine. "Want some wine too?"

"No, thank you, sir."

"And even flight won't help him, in the circumstances. The English will follow, and the poor little man will have to board a ship and sail for Spain or Italy, and that will be the end of the war—one hundred years of war, my boy, one hundred years of war. Or almost. And all France will be English, and the Duke of Bedford will rule us all until the English king is of age. He is a baby now. Would you rather have a baby for your king or a half-wit?"

"A half-wit—if he's a French half-wit," Bertrand de Poulengy said hotly, "but is the dauphin a half-wit, sir?"

"Well, if he isn't, he's pretty well near it. His own mother used to say that he's mad and utterly unfit to rule, but then one should take that with a grain of salt perhaps. Queen Isabeau was not a very nice lady, God rest her soul. She spent money right and left on luxuries, and that's one of the reasons why her son is impoverished, and with him the whole country. There are some who say she really ruined France."

"There is a prophecy by somebody, I think, that a woman would ruin France . . ." Young Bertrand cleared his throat. ". . . and that another woman would save her. Have you heard of that, sir?"

"Yes, yes, there are always prophecies of such kind when a country is in a bad way. Queen Isabeau certainly fits the first part of it, but . . . good Lord, Bertrand, you don't think that country bumpkin out there in the waiting room is the other, do you? Do you? Because if you do, you're considerably madder than our beloved dauphin."

"I don't know what to think, sir", Bertrand de Poulengy replied soberly. "That's why I'd like you to have a look at her yourself."

"Bertrand! Don't tell me you can believe such a story! There are hundreds and perhaps thousands of such girls, hysterical little geese who feel they are called to do great things. You haven't fallen in love with her, have you?"

The young man flushed. "Certainly not, sir, and all I want is for you to get your own impression of this particular hysterical little goose."

"And don't be so touchy, confound you. Why, I really think she's bewitched you or something."

"I don't think she's a witch", Bertrand said thoughtfully. "I have been thinking about that too, and so has Jean de Metz . . ."

"Our clear-headed Jean! You don't mean he has fallen for that nonsense as well!"

"Jean says he knows the girl has got a good reputation in Domrémy." Bertrand was quite unruffled this time. "She's devout and receives the sacraments regularly, so there seems to be no reason why she should be a witch. And there is another thing, sir. The soldiers at the gate were having a quarrel, and some of them were swearing at the top of their voices. The girl walked up to them and told them to stop offending God. They stopped at once. I saw and heard it all from the window of the armory."

"Dominating, overbearing vixen", the captain said with a shrug. "You'll meet quite a number of them, believe me. Big-boned, hefty country girl, I suppose, with muscular arms and a temper."

Bertrand concealed a smile. "Why not judge for yourself, sir?" he suggested.

The captain crashed his fist on the table. "And so I will, by God," he swore, "if only to show you and Jean de Metz how I'm dealing with such a brat. Shove her in."

That was what the young man had been waiting for. He was up and out of the tower room in a flash. A few moments later he returned with Joan, and Captain de Baudricourt stared at her utterly surprised.

The "big-boned, hefty country girl with muscular arms and a temper" turned out to be a girl of little over five foot one or two, slim but wiry, with long, black hair and a pair of lively black eyes. She was wearing a red smock and skirt, rather shabby and patched in a few places, and she was beaming.

The captain began to twist his beard. Before he could say anything, the girl spoke up.

"Good morning, sir captain", she said, curtseying a little. "I have come to deliver a message to you. Please, let me have a horse and armor and a few men to accompany me to the gentle dauphin."

"A horse, armor, and a few men", Baudricourt repeated ironically. "Is that all?"

"Yes, sir captain, but it should be a good horse, please. The armor needn't be so good—not like yours. Just give me what any of your soldiers are wearing. I'll get better armor later from the gentle dauphin."

"Oh, you will, will you?" Baudricourt leaned back. "Now, look here, my girl," he said, "what is the object of this tomfoolery? Who's put you up to it?"

"My Voices put me up to it," Joan said cheerfully, "but it's no foolery of any kind. You want France to be saved, don't you?"

"Voices", Baudricourt said contemptuously. "Voices! Whatever next? And France may be in a bad way, but it hasn't come to that yet, that we have to arm our girls."

"If I don't save France," Joan said politely, "who's going to do it? Will you do it, sir captain?"

Bertrand de Poulengy stared at the ceiling. Baudricourt, glancing at him, saw that he was trying very hard to stifle a grin. He became angry.

"I can't do it," he said coldly, "because I am not powerful enough—I, the commander of this fortress, with three hundred men-at-arms under my command. So how can *you* expect to do anything, may I ask? Go back to your parents and be a good girl. Pray for your country, that's the best you can do, and leave men's work to men. Now—go."

"I *am* praying," Joan said quietly, "much more than you do, sir captain. But praying isn't only asking for something or thanking for something or praising God. It is also listening to God and to his saints."

"So now you're trying to teach me theology", Baudricourt snapped.

"No, sir captain. I'm trying to tell you where my

Voices come from. You said you wanted to know who put me up to it, didn't you?"

"Ah, yes, your Voices", Baudricourt sneered. "Your uncle or cousin or whatever he is told me about your hearing voices at your previous visit, if I remember right-fully . . ."

"Yes, sir captain, and he told you that my Voices demanded of me to save Orléans from the English, and you laughed at him because Orléans was not in danger then. It is in danger now, isn't it, sir captain? My Voices were right, weren't they, sir captain?"

"See what I mean, sir?" Bertrand de Poulengy asked softly.

"You be quiet", the captain snapped. "All right, so Orléans is in danger. The English are besieging the city. So what do you intend to do?"

"I shall raise the siege", Joan said promptly.

"Is that so?" Baudricourt almost burst with sarcasm. "And how do you suppose to set about that?"

"I don't know yet", Joan replied simply. "My Voices told me to do it. They'll tell me how, when the time comes."

"Certainly, certainly, no doubt about it at all. And then?"

"Then I must lead the gentle dauphin to Rheims, to have him crowned in the cathedral."

Baudricourt jumped to his feet. "Good Lord. You are mad, girl, insane, stark raving mad. Crown the dauphin! Who do you think you are?"

"I'm Joan d'Arc from Domrémy", said the girl. "Surely you know that."

Baudricourt made an effort to control himself. "You mean to say you want me to believe that you can achieve all that—you, a little girl that I could crush between two fingers?"

"My Voices told me to do it, so it must be possible", Joan said.

"Who are those voices of yours? Things you are hearing in a dream, I suppose."

"Oh, no, sir captain. I'm always wide awake when I hear them. I'm even more awake then than I am now, talking to you."

"But they don't seem to have any names of their own", Baudricourt jeered.

"Yes, they have", Joan replied eagerly. "They belong to Saint Catherine and to Saint Margaret and to Saint Michael, the archangel."

Baudricourt blew up his cheeks. "Holy terror", he said.

"There's nothing terrifying about it", Joan said sweetly. "They're all creatures of the good God, aren't they, though I do admit I was a little terrified at the beginning, when I did not know what it was all about. But Saint Michael told me to have courage and God would help me. He told me so several times, when he saw that I was afraid and when I told him that I couldn't ride and that I knew nothing about how to conduct war."

"And now you know all about that, I suppose?"

"No, but I know I shall be told what to do."

Baudricourt had had enough. "It's all nonsense," he exploded, "nonsense from the beginning to the end. A girl in a red skirt wants to save France, raise the siege of Orléans, crown the dauphin in Rheims, and she has war-counsel with a couple of saints and an archangel for that purpose. She doesn't know how to ride or how to conduct war, naturally, but she'll be told what to do by voices of some kind. That'll do, my girl, that's all and more than I can swallow in one gulp. Off with you, and the quicker the better."

Joan nodded. "You have refused me for the second time. My Voices told me you would, although you know now that Orléans is in danger as I told you it would be. When I come to you for the third time, you won't refuse me any more, but it's a great pity that you're delaying my departure so long."

There was a deep anxiety in her voice—or was it only impatience?

Baudricourt wanted to make another sarcastic remark and found he could not. There was something about that girl, he thought. He could not fathom it. Was it a kind of dignity? Absurd, of course. She was a little village girl with a patched skirt; he had known them by the thousand. And yet . . . she *had* dignity. And that was not all, either. She was so desperately in earnest. For one short moment he could almost believe her, but there was that young idiot Bertrand waiting for just that. . . .

Abruptly Baudricourt waved her to go.

She turned and walked away. In the door she turned once more. He could no longer see her face, for she was standing in the shadow, but her voice rang deep and clear like a bell. "This very day the troops of the gentle dauphin are suffering a great defeat. You will hear about it in nine days' time. On the tenth day I shall be back, and then you will grant me what I have asked for."

She was gone before Baudricourt could reply.

Poulengy stepped forward. "Sir . . ."

"What is it?" Baudricourt snapped.

"Sir, when you are sending her to the dauphin, I want your permission to accompany her."

"When I am sending her? I? I shall do nothing of the kind. I . . ."

"And Jean de Metz will want to go, too, sir. We'll take a couple of servants with us. That's all the Maid wants, anyway."

"Whom did you say?"

"The Maid. That's what they're calling her—the soldiers, the people in town, everybody."

"Parcel of lunatics, all of you." Baudricourt turned away and clanked over to the window, his hands folded on his back.

Down in the courtyard small groups of soldiers were talking to each other. Some of them saw the the girl coming out of the tower gate. There was some nudging, and Baudricourt expected the usual grinning and joking that went with the sight of a young girl. Instead, the soldiers stepped back to let her through, and some of them even touched their helmets with their halberds as if she were a military leader.

"Lunatics", Baudricourt repeated.

3

A HORSE FOR JOAN

THE NINTH DAY seemed to pass just as uneventfully as the eight days before it. Baudricourt always had his meals together with his junior officers. He noticed a certain expectancy on their part and he teased them about it, although he himself felt just a little uneasy. That uneasiness vanished when, after the evening meal, the heavy gates of the castle were closed and everybody began to settle down for the night, except, of course, the guards on the watchtowers.

"No news", he said. "The famous ninth day gone and no news. What did I tell you, young Bertrand? And you, Jean? That'll teach you, I hope, not to fall for that kind of rubbish in the future."

The two young officers looked glum.

Baudricourt felt that he could afford to be good-natured about it.

"Don't let it worry you too much", he said. "Better, older, and wiser men than you have been deceived by such tricks. Let's go to bed."

He had scarcely finished speaking when there was a trumpet call from the north tower, a single blast.

"Not an attack—just one man approaching", Baudricourt said.

"The message", said Poulengy. "The message about the defeat."

Baudricourt stamped his foot. "A message, yes. But that's all we know. As you are so eager, Bertrand, go down and see who it is and what it is about."

"Certainly, sir." Poulengy ran. A few minutes later he came back with a tired-looking man of about forty. "The Sieur Laurent, sir captain, clerk in the service of the royal household."

"Sit down, Sieur Laurent", Baudricourt said. "You look as if you had a hard ride."

"I had, sir captain. Worse still, I have to report very bad news."

Poulengy and Jean de Metz exchanged glances.

Baudricourt bit his lip. "Speak up, man", he said.

"We're soldiers, and, God knows, soldiers in this country are getting accustomed to bad news. What is it this time?"

"A grave defeat, sir captain. It is very much to be feared that Orléans is lost."

Baudricourt swore.

"That's right", Poulengy said. "Get rid of it now, sir. Mustn't swear tomorrow when the Maid will be here again."

"Shut up, you young donkey. Now then, Sieur Laurent, what happened? No, wait a minute. Give him a goblet of wine first, Jean. He can do with it."

Laurent accepted it gratefully, wiped his mouth with the back of his hand, and told his story.

"We had news that a convoy of three hundred carts and wagons was under way to the English forces besieging Orléans—food for the troops, sent by the Duke of Bedford himself. Herrings, most of it; the confounded Godons love 'em. A strong detachment of soldiers was escorting the transport. Now that seemed wonderful news to us. Food is terribly scarce in Orléans, and here the enemy himself was bringing it to us, if we could beat the escort. Three hundred carts and wagons—and not only would we have them, the Godons would be deprived of them! It was too good an opportunity to miss, so Count Clermont, our general, decided to march."

"Most unusual", Baudricourt remarked drily. "Count Clermont is a cautious man, I'm told."

"Cautious only in the wrong moments", Laurent said

with a bitter smile. "These are not my words", he added hastily. "It's what the noble Dunois said about him."

"The noble Dunois and I are usually of the same opinion," Baudricourt said, "and he's the best soldier in France and Burgundy, I'm sure."

"We left Blois, where Count Clermont has his headquarters," Laurent went on, "but we soon heard that the escort of the food transport was two thousand strong and under the command of John Fastolf, one of the best commanders of the Godons. So the general sent a message to the noble Dunois to make a sortie from Orléans."

"Good idea—if it's timed well enough", Baudricourt said.

"Yes, sir captain. The noble Dunois fell in with it and sent half his force, almost fifteen hundred men, under La Hire. . . ."

"La Hire! There's a soldier for you. Not as much brain as Dunois and not so nobly born as some families I could name, but a real fighter. How could it go wrong?"

"You mentioned the reason yourself, sir captain—the timing. La Hire marched more quickly than we did, and he could have caught the English by surprise, but an orderly arrived from Count Clermont forbidding him to attack until our forces had arrived too. La Hire cursed and cursed . . ."

"I can well imagine it. Nobody in the whole of Europe knows so many swear words. His tongue must be made of sulphur and brimstone."

". . . but he had to obey. The English, of course, immediately dug in, as they always do, made a sort of castle out of the very carts and wagons and built palisades with the archers' pikes. And still our troops had not arrived. La Hire's officers were hopping mad, seeing the English fortifications grow, and finally he could hold them no longer and they attacked, orders or no orders. They were hungry! They wanted the food, and they resented the English archers standing behind the wall of pikes, mocking them."

Baudricourt sighed heavily. "The same stupidity as at half a dozen other encounters. We never learn. They attacked on horseback, of course, and ran straight against the oblique pikes, impaling themselves."

"Exactly, and the ground was full of fallen horses and unseated knights. They were armed too heavily to rise on their own, and no one was there to help them up. The Godon archers just shot them off, one after the other, like so many sitting ducks. When we arrived, the battle was as good as lost, and Count Clermont was so angry about the attack against his explicit orders that he did nothing to save the rest of La Hire's men. Only about five hundred of them managed to escape. We withdrew—and the English are eating and the Orléanese are tightening their belts."

Laurent gave a bitter laugh. "They're calling it the Battle of the Herrings", he said. "I'm as good a Frenchman as anyone, but I'm beginning to think that we must be deserted by the good God that such things can happen to us. Count Clermont—Dunois—La Hire—all of them military men of courage and skill and experience, and look what happened! By all the saints, if a kitchen maid had led us, we wouldn't have done worse."

"And we might have done better", Bertrand de Poulengy said.

Baudricourt stared at him. "I know what you mean, young rascal, and, by the seven-horned devil, you may be right, too."

"The Maid was right", Bertrand said gravely.

Laurent looked at them both, puzzled.

"There is a girl here", Baudricourt explained with a somewhat embarrassed smile. "She thinks she has been chosen by Saint Michael and—who else was it?"

"Saint Margaret and Saint Catherine", Jean de Metz assisted.

"That's right. The girl thinks she has been chosen by them to save France. She wants me to send her to the dauphin, dressed as a soldier. She's crazy, of course."

"I don't agree", Bertrand de Poulengy said coura-geously.

"Neither do I", Jean de Metz chimed in.

"There you are", Baudricourt grinned sheepishly. "My two subordinates believe in her, and I will admit that she told me nine days ago that I would get the news about another defeat today." He tugged at his beard. "What would you do in my place?"

"I'd send her to the dauphin", cried Laurent. "She can't make things worse than they are. She may be as crazy as you think she is or she may be what your young officers seem to believe she is. In any case, things are so bad that nothing, absolutely nothing, should remain untried."

Bertrand de Poulegny and Jean de Metz stared at their captain with anxious expectation.

He decided to show firmness of character and the superior wisdom of experience. "I shall sleep over it", he said, to their utter disgust. "Now, Bertrand, see to it that the Sieur Laurent gets a good bed and some food. He's had a long ride. Good night."

Baudricourt stalked away. He was well aware of the fact that the two young commanders were furious with him. Let them be furious. They did not have a reputation to lose as he had. It would not do at all if they'd regard him at the dauphin's court in Chinon as a fool ready to believe anything. Not that it mattered so very much what the dauphin thought—if he thought anything at all—but there was La Trémoïlle and Regnault de Chartres and others whose judgment counted for something. Besides, there were always half a dozen commanders who would be only too glad if *they* were in charge of the fortress of Vaucouleurs instead of that superstitious fool of a Baudricourt. There were times when it was much better not to expose oneself, and this was one of them, no doubt.

No, he would have to think it over very carefully. Very carefully.

But what if the girl really was what she thought she was? What if those voices she always talked about really were the voices of the saints? She looked honest enough. It was difficult to conceive that she was trying to deceive him. She wasn't the type at all. Or was she?

He went to bed still debating with himself.

Tomorrow she would turn up again, that much was certain. And he would have to admit that she had been right about the confounded defeat—just as she had been right about the imminent siege of Orléans when she was here for the first time.

If only there were ways and means to find out whether she really was a messenger of the saints. How could he take such a thing on faith? Faith in whom, anyway? A little girl, sixteen or seventeen years of age, eighteen at the most, a little girl in a patched red skirt?

The idea occurred to him to pray to Saint Michael, Saint Margaret and—who was the other?—Saint Catherine, that's right. Pray to them and ask them to guide him.

Quite absurd, of course. You couldn't just talk to them and ask them for a sign or something, could you?

Nevertheless, he prayed.

He awoke and sat up with a jerk. Somebody was shaking him. It was Etienne, his personal valet.

"What's the matter?" he spluttered. "An attack? Where's the enemy? How many . . ."

"There's no attack, sir, but . . ."

"What time is it? Never mind, I can see it's very early, just a little after dawn. What the devil are you waking me for?"

"The Maid has arrived, sir."

Baudricourt bellowed with rage. "Can't she wait at least until I'm up and dressed and had my breakfast? The Maid, the Maid, everything I hear these days is the Maid. . . ."

"She's in the courtyard, sir, on her horse, and . . ."

"On her horse, did you say? But she can't ride. Who gave her the horse, anyway?"

"I don't know, sir, but for someone who can't ride she is riding extremely well, sir."

"You donkey", said Baudricourt. "Preposterous donkey." He jumped out of bed, threw a woolen cloak around his body, and stepped to the window. "Amazing", he said, stupefied, and began to twist his beard violently.

The boyish creature down there in the yard, with its hair cropped in a military way so that it formed a complete circle just above the ears, and dressed like a boy, too, in black hose, black doublet and a black riding cloak, was the Maid, but if Etienne had not mentioned that she was here, Baudricourt might not have recognized her.

She was sitting on a large roan. The roan had a temper and was rearing, and she was laughing and swinging the horse around so that a few soldiers had to jump like frogs to get away from its hooves. She was mastering the brute like a seasoned cavalrist. There, it was quiet now, and she patted it.

"She *can* ride", Baudricourt thought. "She has lied to

me." But he dismissed the thought the very next moment. He knew how that girl had been brought up. No one was keeping riding horses in Domrémy or any other village in Lorraine. At best the girl might have sat a few times on the back of an ox. And however crazy she might be, she wasn't a liar. She just wasn't. But, then, how was it that she could ride?

He turned away. "Right", he said in a thick voice. "Go and tell her to wait for me in the hall. I will give her a letter for the dauphin."

To his surprise, Etienne beamed all over his wrinkled face.

"What are you so glad about, you silly old idiot?"

"Oh, sir, we all hoped you'd help the Maid to save the country."

"Get out", Baudricourt bellowed. "And when you've told her, get some breakfast for me, and for her, too."

Etienne vanished like a shot, and Baudricourt splashed himself a bit, dressed, and, after a Pater and an Ave, communicated with Saint Michael, Saint Margaret, and Saint Catherine. "She can ride", he said. "She can ride as well as I can and maybe better. I did ask you for a sign that she was genuine, and I think this is it. Farm girls don't know how to ride war-horses, and, if they did, they couldn't ride like this girl, so I think you had a hand in this. Now I'm going to risk it because I'd rather lose my reputation with the Duke of La Trémoïlle and the other bigwigs at court than with you. Amen."

Then he went to the tower room to write that letter.

It was the most difficult letter he had ever written, and yet somehow it seemed to flow as easily as if he had just wanted to send the dauphin birthday greetings.

He was sealing it when Bertrand de Poulengy and Jean de Metz came in, both dressed for a journey. He frowned a little; they did take a good deal for granted. Then he decided to take it for granted, too.

"You have my permission to accompany the Maid", he said crisply, and now these two started beaming just as Etienne had. He stared at them hard. "I want you to swear an oath that you will take her safely to the dauphin's headquarters in Chinon," he said, "and that you will protect her with your lives."

The two young men swore the oath, still beaming.

"Very well", Baudricourt said. "Now let's all have breakfast. Show the Maid in here." He did not say "shove her in" this time.

Bertrand de Poulengy ran to fetch her and she appeared, like a slim youth who walked in his new clothes as if he had never worn skirts in his life.

"I bid you welcome", Baudricourt said courteously. "Please sit down and have breakfast with us." He felt somewhat embarrassed in the presence of one who was a personal friend and instrument of saints and of an archangel. "I'd better get accustomed to it", he thought. "I'll meet them all one day, myself, on the other side . . . if I'm lucky."

Joan accepted the invitation as the most natural thing, and a moment later Etienne and two other servants appeared with the breakfast dishes, bread, cheese, a little fruit, and wine. It was Lent.

"Better eat a hearty meal", Baudricourt said a little gruffly. "I'm told they're eating very little at the dauphin's court."

"I'm not going there in order to feed well", Joan said merrily.

Bertrand de Poulengy poured her a goblet of wine, and she soaked a piece of bread in it and ate it. She did not touch anything else.

Baudricourt sighed. "I don't know whether you realize that there are a good many highwaymen and deserters lurking on the way to Chinon", he said. "It might be better to take a stronger escort, or to postpone the journey a little."

"I'd rather go now than tonight," she replied, "rather today than tomorrow, and rather tomorrow than the day after."

"*Tenax propositi*", murmured Baudricourt, who had studied Latin for a couple of years when his parents still hoped that he might become a priest. "In other words, you want to stick to it, eh? I only hope you won't encounter hostile men of war."

"For men of war I care nothing", she said calmly. "The road lies smooth before my feet; and if so be I encounter armed enemies, the Lord God will open a way for me through the midst of them, that I may go to my lord dauphin, since for that I was born."

It came to Baudricourt that she had taken for granted

his permission to go, even before he had given it to her. Somebody must have shorn her hair; again somebody must have given her these clothes. He glanced at Bertrand and Jean de Metz. It was not too difficult to guess who that somebody or these somebodies had been. "I wonder a little", he said, "what you're going to tell the dauphin, how you're going to convince him of your . . . your mission."

"I have no idea," Joan said cheerfully, "but I'll know it when I'm there. I'm always told enough about what I have to know."

"Where did you get that horse?" Baudricourt asked.

Bertrand de Poulengy replied for her: "I bought it from the dealer in the town."

"What did he charge you?"

"A fairly stiff price, sixteen francs."

Baudricourt gave another sigh. "I'll pay it back to you", he said. "After all, this is my affair. Who bought those clothes?"

"I did", Jean de Metz owned up.

"You'll get your money back too."

"You have all been very good to me," Joan said, "and God will not forget it." She rose. "I want to go now."

They followed her to the courtyard. A few servants on horseback were holding the three mounts in readiness. Durand Laxart was there too, and Joan embraced him and whispered: "When you see my parents, tell them I love them, but God must be served first."

Durand nodded. Tears were trickling down his cheeks.

Baudricourt gave Bertrand de Poulengy the letter he had written to the dauphin. "Deliver it to his own hands, if you can manage it," he said, "and I hope you'll get through safely."

Joan heard his last words. "Be very sure that none of us will meet any evil fate on this journey", she said. She mounted so quickly that none of the men was in time to help her.

"She looks like a warrior", Baudricourt thought. "A warrior, not a soldier. If angels and archangels could have children, they might well look like her. Where did I have my eyes that I didn't see it earlier?"

Their eyes met.

A little to his own surprise, Baudricourt gave her a military salute, as if she were his superior. "Perhaps she is", he thought. "Either she is—or I'm the biggest idiot in France." But only his mind still tried to be doubtful; his heart did not.

He cleared his throat. "Go," he said, "go, and come what may."

She smiled down to him, and suddenly he knew with an almost terrifying certainty that he had done the right thing, that he had been tested and stood the test. He felt relieved and at the same time deeply moved. A moment longer, and he would slobber like that peasant, that yokel of a Durand Laxart.

"Lower the drawbridge", he roared. "Up the portcullis. Get a move on, you there."

Half a dozen soldiers jumped into action.

Joan made the sign of the Cross—a wide, sweeping gesture that seemed to linger in the air when her hand had already gone back to the reins. A moment later the hooves of her horse were clattering across the drawbridge. Bertrand de Poulengy and Jean de Metz followed, and two servants brought up the rear.

4

JOAN IS PUT TO A TEST

THE LITTLE CAVALCADE arrived at Chinon on March 6, 1429, the fourth Sunday in Lent, Laetare.

Bertrand de Poulengy tried to convince the officer in charge of the castle gate that he had to deliver a personal letter to the dauphin. The officer laughed. "Not the ghost of a chance", he said. "With all due respect to the good commander of Vaucouleurs, bigger and more powerful men than he have tried that kind of thing. No one can see the dauphin except on recommendation of the Duke de La Trémoïlle or another of the great gentlemen at court. *They* haven't given you any letters, I suppose? They haven't? I thought so. Best I can do for you is to dispatch a man to the royal suite and deliver your letter there. Whether the dauphin is going to see it or not I have no idea—and, if he's going to see it, I can't guarantee you that he's going to read it. So give that scribbly thing to me or don't, it's all the same to me."

"Give it to him", Joan said curtly, and Bertrand obeyed.

They took lodgings at an inn nearby, and for two long days nothing happened at all except that Joan was stared at in the church where she went to hear Mass.

On the third day a number of courtiers paid a visit to the inn to have a meal there. Soon it became clear that this was only a pretext. A great deal of inquiring and whispering was going on, and Joan was stared at until she silently withdrew to the dingy little room the landlady had put at her disposal.

Then rumors began to spread through the town, and groups of people appeared, curious to get a glimpse of "The Maid". At first there were only dozens or twenties, but soon their numbers swelled to hundreds.

"Everybody seems interested except the one for whom I have come", Joan said impatiently, but even she knew that it was no good trying to enter the castle without being asked. She released her impatience in prayer.

One of the queen's woman attendants appeared, "to
have a look at the girl who wants to be a soldier", as she
put it. Joan would not see her, and she departed in a
huff.

Two clerics came, followed by the dauphin's confessor, and the three of them talked to Joan for half an hour
and then departed again. Her last word to them was:
"There is so much delay; and French blood must flow
because of it."

Suddenly, the next evening, the message came that
her presence was asked for at the castle. Bertrand de
Poulengy and Jean de Metz rode with her to the gate.
The invitation was for her alone, and she alone was
allowed to pass.

Inside, in the large courtyard, a number of soldiers
were waiting. Their attitude did not show much disci-
pline; several of them were slightly drunk, and one of
these, a huge, red-haired fellow, asked fairly loudly: "Is
that the famous Maid?" The others tried to silence him,
but he burst into a stream of vile abuse.

Joan looked at him. She was very pale, and her voice
was trembling a little as she said: "You offend God—you
who will die so soon?"

The man gaped at her. Before he could make a reply,
she dismounted and walked straight into the castle, where
two lackeys with torches led her up a gloomy staircase
and into one of the small audience rooms. The room
was empty. Its furniture consisted of a wooden dais with
a single gilt chair and a canopy above it. Its only light

consisted of the two torches which the lackeys left behind as they vanished through another door.

"Most exciting", said the dauphin eagerly. "She should be here by now. I wonder what she's like. You haven't seen her yet, have you, my dear archbishop?"

Archbishop Regnault of Chartres shrugged his shoulders. "No, I have not, Your Highness. But as your father confessor seems to be of the opinion that there is nothing directly wrong with her, I feel no need to interfere with the amusement Your Highness wishes to indulge in."

The dauphin rubbed his bulbous nose. "Amusement", he repeated. "I don't know about that. She may be what I've been hoping for, I mean, she may be the answer to what . . . never mind, but if she is what she ought to be from what Baudricourt writes in his letter, then she's no mere amusement. And if she is not what he thinks she is, then I won't find it amusing at all, and I shall certainly give Baudricourt a piece of my mind."

The archbishop smiled drily. "The mind is a precious possession", he said. "Few people can afford to give pieces of it away."

The dauphin giggled. "That's your polite way of telling me that I'm stupid, isn't it? No, no, I'm not offended. I know I'm stupid—up to a point, that is. I always feel that I'm far more intelligent than some people credit me for, or far less, but never just as they think I am. Vanity, I suppose. By the way, my dear archbishop, I'm sorry to have to ask you again, but I must have three thousand francs."

"Your Highness . . ."

"I know it's awful, but what can I do? The queen must have a new dress; she flatly refuses to participate in any state occasions unless she has one, and I can't really blame her, you know. And I have nothing with which to pay the salaries of the people in the kitchen next week."

"I would much prefer, if Your Highness saw fit, to ask the Duke de La Trémoïlle . . ."

"Impossible, my dear archbishop. I had to sign away six of my castles to him on previous occasions. This time he would ask for Chinon, and then he could throw me out whenever he wants to—and, knowing him, I think he may want to one fine day."

" . . . or one of your other great nobles—the Sieur de Gaucourt, for instance . . ."

"I still owe him his pay as a general of the army!"

"Three thousand francs", the archbishop murmured. "Your Highness has a very exaggerated opinion of my funds."

"Make it two thousand then, or even fifteen hundred. I'll talk to the queen, but I can't let the little people go hungry, can I? What is this noise going on outside?"

"It's the Duke de La Trémoïlle's voice, I believe", said the archbishop. "He sounds rather angry."

"He always does," the dauphin nodded, "and what is more, he is."

A lackey entered. "His Grace the Duke de La—". He

did not get any farther. The duke's huge arm pushed him out of the way, and La Trémoïlle came in like a charging bull, an enormously large man with a brick-red face. "'Evening, Your Highness", he growled. "I have come to enquire about something I heard this morning. If it's not true, well and good, but if it is, I shall wash my hands of this court."

The dauphin stepped back a little. "A nice beginning," he said, "but then you always have such nice beginnings, my dear duke. What is this all about?"

The duke was breathing heavily. "I'm told you have the intention to put what is left of your army under the command of a petticoat", he said. "It's so ridiculous I could scarcely get the sentence out, but, with Your Highness, one never knows, does one? Well, is it true?"

"I don't know", the dauphin replied cautiously. "How could I know? I haven't seen the girl yet, if she is what you mean by that somewhat undignified expression."

"She is. And she's here", the duke bellowed.

"Excellent", exclaimed the dauphin. "I've been waiting for that. For once you're bringing me good news, my dear duke."

"You won't see her", La Trémoïlle raged. "Surely it is below your dignity to receive that kind of rabble, let alone . . ."

"Now, now, my dear duke", the dauphin interrupted. "You mustn't call her names, really you mustn't. The archbishop wouldn't like it, I'm sure, not if the girl is what she may well be."

"I must beg Your Highness to leave me out of this", the archbishop said hastily. "I have formed no opinion. . . ."

"Exactly", the dauphin said. "The archbishop has not formed an opinion, so you shouldn't either. Nor should I."

"You won't see her", La Trémoïlle insisted.

"If I don't see her, how can I know what she is like?" the dauphin replied innocently.

The duke shrugged his huge shoulders. "Very well, then, see her, if you must, but don't do anything rash, or . . ."

"Or you'll wash your hands, I know", the dauphin nodded.

"Your Highness appears to be in a rather ferocious mood," the duke jeered, "but where would you be if I withdrew my hand? And with me most of the great names, too, the few that are still on your side?"

"Good heavens," the dauphin said, "if I didn't know that you *like* threatening people, and especially me, I'd think you are afraid of the Maid. Are you, my dear duke?"

"I'm afraid of nobody", La Trémoïlle declared disdainfully.

"Excellent", the dauphin said. "Then you will beat the English for me, won't you. General Talbot and Colonel Glasdale and Fastolf and, of course, their Burgundian allies too. What are we waiting for, my dear duke?" But he backed away when the enormous duke walked up to

him. "Careful now", he warned. "If you hit me, you'll
lose your head, so keep off."

"You wouldn't find anybody who could take me to
task for it", the duke said angrily. "No one would dare.
Besides, if they want to accuse me of having hit the king,
they first would have to prove that you are the king. And
you're not, you know. You haven't been crowned with
the Crown of Charlemagne; you haven't been anointed
with the holy oil, have you?"

The archbishop thought it was time to interfere. "Your
Grace is not seriously suggesting, I hope, that the right-
ful king of France is to be found in the enemy's camp?
The king of England . . ."

". . . hasn't been crowned and anointed either, as far
as I know", La Trémoïlle fell in. "His claim to the French
crown is as yet nothing more than a claim, but there are
times when it may be well to keep an open mind. In any
case, what is going on here in Chinon is a stupid com-
edy. Nothing royal about it! Anybody, just anybody, at
court would make a better and more presentable king
than this wretched young man here."

There was a pause.

The dauphin, pale as a sheet, gave a forced smile. "I
know I'm not much to look at", he said in an unsteady
voice. "I can see myself every day in the mirror when I
shave, and I don't like what I see. I don't look like a
warrior, do I, with my thin arms and spindly legs? I
don't look like a sage either, and I know I'm not a saint.
And France more than ever needs a king who is at least

one of these three things and preferably all three of them."

"Well said, Your Highness", the archbishop assented.

"And yet," the dauphin went on, "I wonder whether the Maid wouldn't know who I am, if she came in here."

The archbishop smiled. "A child of six would know that neither the noble duke nor I could be the dauphin. Everybody knows that the dauphin is very young, and His Grace is nearing sixty . . ."

"Fifty-four", La Trémoïlle protested scornfully.

". . . and I am fifty-two and dressed in these robes", the archbishop concluded. "It's a simple matter of elimination."

"I tell you what we'll do", the dauphin said eagerly. "We'll let the entire court assemble here, and *then* we'll see whether she'll know which is me. Wait." He tugged at the cord of a bell suspended just behind him.

Two lackeys entered. "I want the court assembled here", the dauphin ordered. "All the nobles waiting anywhere, the ladies, the petitioners—everybody."

"He's found another game to play", La Trémoïlle said with a shrug. "He'll never grow up."

The room began to fill. Most of the nobles and their ladies gave the dauphin a somewhat careless bow before they arranged themselves in the semicircle prescribed by royal etiquette.

The dauphin clapped his hands. "Listen, everybody," he said, "the Maid will be coming in here. I know I don't have to explain to you whom I mean by that; you always know everything before I do. She is here now. His Grace the Duke de La Trémoïlle has just announced her arrival to me."

The brick-red-faced giant glared at him.

"There seems to be some doubt about her claims", the dauphin proceeded.

"I should say so", exploded the duke.

"There you are," the dauphin said, "so I have decided to put her to test. My Lord de Montigny, you will take my place on the Chair of State and address her as if you were me. It'll be only for a few minutes."

"Just as well, Your Highness", Montigny said, caressing his handsome moustache. "I don't think I could stand such an honor much longer."

Some of the courtiers tittered. The dauphin pretended not to have heard them. Years of misery and humiliation had taught him that the best way to meet insults was to ignore them.

Montigny sat down on the Chair of State, giving a clever imitation of the dauphin's usual attitude of dejectedness, with his arms hanging down lifelessly and his chin sunk on his chest. The courtiers tittered again, of course.

The dauphin slipped into the ranks of the courtiers. "Now!" he said. "Let her enter." Two pages went to fetch her.

Everybody was looking at the door through which the Maid would come in, and thus no one saw the dauphin's true face. For once he forgot the masks he

always wore in public—the mask of boredom, of sullen-
ness, of unnatural, childish hilarity or of morbid dejection.
He stared toward the entrance with rapt expectancy. A
thin red was mounting in his pallid cheeks, and his
hands, behind the broad back of a stately lady-in-waiting,
were folded in a prayer full of hope and yet very near
despair.

As Joan came in there was absolute silence. Some of
the courtiers had seen her before at the inn, but the
majority of the assembly had not, and they were utterly
bewildered, for the same reasons, perhaps, as Captain de
Baudricourt. The Maid who claimed to be sent by God
and his saints was a young girl, smaller than most pages at
court. They would have liked to laugh, but they could
not. Despite her short-cropped hair and her mannish
clothes, there was nothing ridiculous about her. She
seemed never to have worn anything else. And she was
neither overawed by the glittery assembly, nor brash or
brazen.

She walked across the large room, neither as if she
were afraid nor as if it belonged to her, but like one who
has a very definite, businesslike purpose. Now her eyes
fastened on the Lord of Montigny on the Chair of State.

Montigny, too, was a little taken aback, but he was
determined to act his part. He was just going to address
her in a solemn voice when she turned away from him
and glanced at the crowd.

She walked straight into it and stopped before the
dauphin, who stared at her, trembling.

She curtseyed to him. "Gentle dauphin," she said calmly, "I am Joan, whom they call the Maid. The King of Heaven sends me to you with the message that you shall be anointed and crowned in the city of Rheims, and that you shall be the lieutenant of the King of Heaven, who is also the King of France."

There was one more moment of silence; then everybody spoke at the same time.

The dauphin alone held firm and went on with the test. "It is not I who am the dauphin, Joan. There he is", he said, pointing at the Lord of Montigny.

She smiled at him. "In God's name, noble prince, it is you and none other who are the dauphin."

His eyes gleamed. "Come with me, Joan", he said in a hoarse voice.

She followed him to a corner of the room, where they were out of earshot. "I want to believe you", he said. "Can you help me to make me believe you?"

"Sire," she replied, "if I tell you things so secret that God and you alone know about them, will you believe that I am sent by God?"

"I think so", he said breathlessly. "Yes, I think I will believe you then. What is this secret between God and myself?"

"On last All Saints' Day," she said, "you were alone in your oratory in the chapel of the castle of Loches. There and then you requested three things of God."

"That is true", he murmured. "Go on, I beg of you, go on. What were these things?"

"The first request was that it should be God's pleasure to take away your courage in the matter of recovering France, if you were not the true heir, so that you should no longer be the cause of prolonging a war bringing so much suffering in its train."

"Yes . . . yes . . ."

"The second request", Joan continued, "was that you alone should be punished, either through death or any other penance, if the troubles and tribulations that the poor people of France had endured so long were due to your own sins. And the third request was that the people should be forgiven and God's anger appeased, if the sins of the people were the cause of their troubles."

The dauphin seized Joan's hand and led her back to the assembly. "Listen, all of you", he cried. "By my honor and the honor of France, the Maid has been sent by God." Irradiated by faith and joy, his plain face looked almost beautiful.

5

NEW ATTIRE FOR THE MAID

NEWS IN CHINON was abounding. There was no
need to invent rumors and no need to gossip; the
facts themselves were numerous and exciting enough.

Factions formed for and against the Maid. Those
against her called her a subtle little cheat who was set on
an adventurous career and made use of the wretched
dauphin's gullible nature. Those who were for her could
point out that no one could prove that she had lied in
one single case. On the contrary, at her arrival at the
castle she had told a drunken officer who blasphemed

that he would die very soon, and the man had fallen into the moat of the castle that same day and was drowned miserably.

Coincidence, the first group maintained.

But if that was a coincidence, how come that when she had told the dauphin she needed a sword—not just any sword, but a certain weapon that they would find in the vault of the church of Saint Catherine in Fierbois and that they would recognize by five small red crosses on its hilt—the dauphin's messengers had gone to Fierbois and found the sword there? Very old it was, and some of the monks thought it was the one that once, almost seven hundred years before, belonged to the great Charles Martel, who defeated the Arabs in the great battle of Tours and Poitiers and thus saved France and Europe from becoming Muslim!

She might be a witch, the other faction declared. There were some who said that she had told the dauphin certain things that he and God alone knew—but the devil too had ways and means of acquiring information, and it was just like a disciple of the devil to curse a poor soldier so that he fell into a moat and drowned.

Those in favor of the Maid replied that she had never cursed the drunken soldier; on the contrary, it was he who cursed and was well known for being foul-mouthed. She had warned him of his approaching death and thereby given him the opportunity to make his peace with God. Was that the action of one commanded by Satan?

In the meantime, the Maid was installed in a round tower of the castle, and little Louis de Contes, a boy of fifteen, was given her as a page. The dauphin sent Bertrand de Poulengy and Jean de Metz back to Vaucouleurs with a letter of thanks for Captain Robert de Baudricourt. They went with much regret. Both of them wanted to stay with the Maid and fight at her side, once it came to fighting.

However, it did not look as if fighting were to come soon. Despite the Maid's incessant pressing for action, the two factions went on with their wrangling.

In favor of the Maid, apart from the dauphin, was the young Duke of Alençon, who had helped to defend the fortress of Saint Michael against the English, one of the very few places the English had not managed to conquer. He was a young man of twenty-four, and he had a natural feud with the English as well as a national one: his father had been killed by the English king, Henry the Fifth, in single combat during the terrible battle at Agincourt, but not before he had struck the crown off his royal opponent's helmet. D'Alençon—and with him many young and enthusiastic nobles—were as much for Joan as some of the old guard, like the Duke de La Trémoïlle and the Sieur de Gaucourt, were against her.

The old guard was afraid of her. What was France, what was the civilized world coming to, if the great names of ancient lineage were to be subordinate to a young peasant girl? If she was successful, this might well lead to a direct understanding between a crowned dauphin and his simple subjects, between King Charles the Seventh of France and the citizens in the towns, the villagers, the personal subjects of the great nobles. If Joan could come to the king and get a command for the asking, why should the ordinary man hesitate to go straight to the king if he wanted justice done—and go to the king, of course, with complaints against the feudal lords!

And if the Maid failed . . . what a howl of derision would go up on the side of the enemy.

The worst thing was that even now the rumor of a peasant girl from a remote little village in Lorraine who would save France and have the dauphin crowned was spreading like wildfire in all directions. There was no stopping it.

"Exactly", those in favor of the Maid said. "We cannot disappoint the atmosphere of expectancy. If the Maid does not come now, the last shred of hope will be gone, and that will mean disaster."

This was a very serious argument. Two courageous men had slipped out of besieged Orléans and arrived at Chinon to plead for speedy help. They heard about the Maid almost as soon as they arrived. They had even seen her, and now they had gone back to Orléans radiant with hope. Orléans knew. Orléans was waiting for the Maid. The brave defender of the city, Dunois, helped to spread the news. He did not know what to believe, but anything apt to put fresh hope into the weary troops and the half-starved people was more than welcome to him.

Still the two factions went on wrangling with each other, and the dauphin was not strong enough to make a final decision in the face of so much resistance.

Joan demanded a major offensive, with herself as the head of the army. A major offensive . . . when the royal treasury was empty, when the dauphin himself had to borrow small sums to keep his household going! Even so, the High Council might agree—but how could he get those sceptical old men to believe in Joan's divine mission? The fact that she had convinced *him* meant little or nothing to them.

In the end the two factions agreed to call in the Church, as well as the parliament, and the entire royal court proceeded to Poitiers, where the parliament was in session.

Joan's examination took place in a private house, with Archbishop Regnault of Chartres presiding. Present as examiners were many learned priests and monks, including the much feared Inquisitor, Father Turelure of the Dominican order.

The archbishop made it clear that the duty of the members of the assembly was to question the young girl and to give their opinion about her, as a Catholic and as the alleged holder of a divine mission. Then they were to decide whether the dauphin could make use of her services with a good conscience.

Never before had the learned ecclesiastics dealt with

such a candidate for sanctity. If at least some of them thought of Joan as of a country bumpkin with some kind of religious hysteria, they were very quickly set right.

"We are here as representatives of the king", one of the scholarly men began.

"You are here to question me, it seems", she replied, and she added with a faint smile: "I know nothing whatever."

Maître Jean Erault promptly asked: "Then why have you come?"

Her eyes blazed. "Have you paper and ink?" she asked. "Then write this to the English: 'English commanders Suffolk, Glasdale, and de la Pole, I call upon you in the name of the King of Heaven to return to England . . .' "

They stopped her as she was trying to go on with her dictating and began to question her about herself, about the origin of what she conceived to be her mission, and particularly about her Voices.

They quoted from author after author to prove to her why she should not be believed. She replied serenely: "My Lord has more books than you have."

Professor Seguin of the University of Poitiers rose, a thin, sour-faced man. "In what language do your voices speak to you?" he asked. His accent was that of the people of the Limousin, a province not exactly noted for refinement in speech.

"In a better language than yours", she replied, and some of her examiners could not help tittering.

The professor frowned. "Do you believe in God?" he snapped.

"Yes, and better than you do", was the sharp answer.

"Then you must understand", Seguin went on acidly, "that God does not wish us to accept you merely on your own word. We cannot advise the dauphin to put his men-at-arms at your disposal, unless you give us proof that you deserve such a trust."

"In God's name," she exploded, "I have not come to Poitiers to perform signs. Lead me to Orléans, and I will show you the signs for which I am sent." The professor was still thinking of what to ask her next when she went on, her eyes blazing: "Orléans will be relieved. The English will be destroyed and France freed of their presence. The dauphin will be crowned in Rheims, and in due course Paris too will recognize him as its king."

Brother Guillaume Aymerie leaned forward: "You say your Voices tell you that God wishes to free the people of France of their present calamities. But surely if he wishes to free them it is not necessary to have an army at all."

"In God's name," Joan said, "the soldiers will fight and God will give the victory."

In a corner of the room a deep voice said what most of the clerics thought by now: "No one in Holy Orders could have answered better."

It was not an easy thing for these dignified men, who had spent all their lives in learning and teaching, to accept Joan's harsh and almost discourteous answers. Yet none of them showed offense, and Professor Seguin even grinned a little when his colleague Aymerie fared no better in his debate with the Maid than he had done. They were not only learned, they were good and holy men, and, as such, they could recognize the voice of honesty and sincerity. They understood that Joan was not capable of answering them the way she did all on her own, and they all felt the dynamic influence of her personality. They knew that the abruptness of her answers was due to an impatience not of her temper but of the very force that was urging her on. Divine impatience was bursting out of her; just so it would be if she really were an instrument of God and of God's saints, filled with a fire she could not contain.

They closed the examination and, after a secret council, decided to recommend to the dauphin to put his trust in the Maid.

Preparations now started in earnest. The court returned to Chinon and orders were given to all commanders to assemble troops and equipment at Tours.

The Maid, now officially in command of all the armed forces of the dauphin, was given a kind of staff of her own, consisting of the Sieur Jean d'Aulon, a powerfully built knight of almost proverbial strength and honesty, two other officers, two heralds, a number of servants, and, of course, her page, little Louis de Contes, who by now was so devoted to her that he would let himself be quartered for her sake. On her own instruction, a banner was made for her of white silk. Painted on it were a portrait of Christ, angels, and the words JHESUS MARIA. Such, she said, was what her saints had told her the standard should be like. She would carry it herself.

"How can you do that?" they asked her. "You will need your hands when you go into battle."

She answered that it was in order for her to avoid killing anyone with her own hands.

"But we have given you the sword from the church in Fierbois!"

"I was ordered to ask for that sword, not to kill with it. And I would rather go without the sword than without the banner."

She was so sure of what she had to do, and for everything she had a clear, simple answer that left no doubt whatever.

The young Duke of Alençon was delighted with her. He watched her riding a black charger as if she had been born on it; he saw her giving orders to grizzled commanders whose scarred faces lit up when she addressed them. He told his beautiful wife: "To be with her is to be with victory incarnate." But his wife was worried. He was going to war again. She dreamed of his being wounded, killed, taken prisoner. The duke found the right remedy. He took Joan to see her.

Joan smiled at the lovely young noblewoman. "Have no fear, Madame, for I will bring him safely back to you, and in as good condition as he is at present, if not in better."

The Duchess of Alençon looked at her. "I believe you", she said.

One more member of her staff joined her: the Augustinian Friar Jean Pasquerel, thin and frail, but wise and courageous. He was to be her confessor. "I'll be with you whenever you need me and as long as you need me", he said quietly a few minutes after they met.

She went to Blois to be with the troops who assembled there. Here she dictated the letter in which she had been interrupted at her examination in Poitiers. "JHESUS MARIA. King of England, and you, Duke of Bedford, calling yourself Regent of France; William de la Pole, Earl of Suffolk; John Lord Talbot, and you, Thomas Lord Scales, calling yourselves lieutenants of the said Bedford . . . deliver the keys of all the good towns you have taken and violated in France to the Maid who has been sent by God the King of Heaven. . . . Go away, for God's sake, back to your own country; otherwise, await news of the Maid, who will soon visit you to your great detriment!"

A herald was sent off with it to the English lines around Orléans. He did not return. . . .

Here in Blois, Joan also met the High Command of her army: the Marshal Saint-Sévère, the Marshal Gilles de Rais, an adventurous figure, sporting a little beard dyed dark blue, and the Sieur de Gaucourt. And here she met the most ferocious, cantankerous, hot-headed, and grim of all French commanders of the time, the Gascon Etienne de Vignerolles, known to everybody as La Hire.

"Never served under a girl in all my life", La Hire said. "By all the seven archdevils, never thought it would come to that. But I'll be damned and roast in hell if it doesn't amuse me, and it'll serve the blasted Godons right to be defeated by a girl, so I promise you by all the damned souls in . . ."

"Stop", Joan said fiercely. "I want to be your friend, and I know you are a valiant man, but if you wish to march with this army you must give up cursing as from this moment."

La Hire began to laugh. "Every soldier in the entire army is cussing away whenever he feels like it. You can't help that, you know."

"I can and I will", Joan insisted coolly. "There was a soldier who cursed when I first came into the castle of Chinon. Has no one told you what happened to him?"

La Hire had heard of the story and began to rub a long, fiery red scar on his left cheek, as was his habit. "No cussing", he murmured. "By all the . . . I mean, that won't be easy. By all the . . . it's downright impossible. A man must have *something* to swear by."

"You may say 'in the Name of God' ", Joan permitted. "I often say so myself, but only when I mean exactly and solemnly what I say."

La Hire fingered the heavy stick he always carried around with him. His temper was so sharp that he hit out on the slightest provocation, and in such case it was better to do so with a stick than with the sharp blade of his sword. "In the Name of God", he murmured unhappily. "Is that all? Isn't there anything else I could use?"

She grinned at him cheerfully. "You can use anything that isn't sacred or doesn't evoke God's enemies", she said. "Swear by that stick of yours, if you wish. . . ."

La Hire grinned back. "It's an idea."

"And I want you to tell it to the troops", Joan went on. "No one else is better fitted for it."

La Hire grunted (fortunately, what he grunted was not clear) and set out to do it. In front of Joan and her staff and almost three thousand troops he roared: "Attention. Here's an order of the Maid. There'll be no more cursing in the army."

Every soldier knew that La Hire himself did more cursing than anybody else, and there was a roar of laughter.

La Hire raised his stick. "By my stick," he bellowed, "if I find anybody cursing, using foul names or suchlike, I'll bash his damn . . . I mean I'll bash his no-good head in. This is an *order*, do you hear me, you . . . you . . . in the Name of God, if I'd say what you are, I'd blaspheme myself, but that's what you are."

He tramped off.

Now Joan herself spoke up. "Before we set out," she said, "I want every single man to go to confession and to receive the Blessed Sacrament. If any man refuses to do so, he will not march with us."

No one was laughing now.

On Wednesday, May 27, 1429, the little army began to move. The object of the operation was not yet to raise the siege of Orléans, but only to get a large transport of food into the beleaguered city. The dauphin could not hope to get many more troops together, and thus much depended upon the help of both the garrison and the citizens of Orléans, who needed food urgently to get back into shape.

Joan was wearing full armor: cuirass, arm pieces, leg pieces, and helmet, all made of polished steel, "white armor", as it was called at the time.

The evening before, she and every man in the army had gone to confession. Now, at dawn, they all went to hear Mass. Only then the march began.

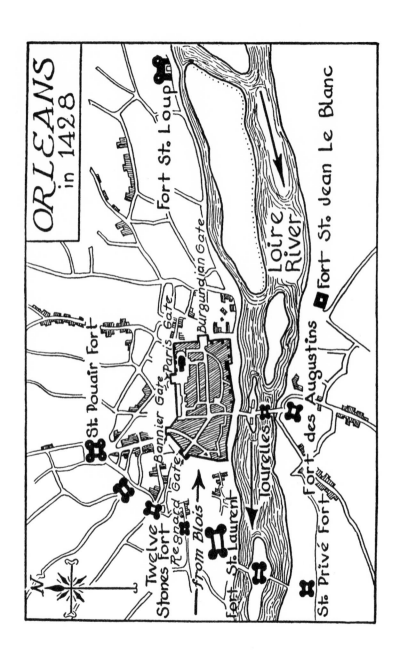

ORLEANS in 1428

Fort St. Loup

Loire River

Fort St. Jean Le Blanc

Burgundian Gate

St. Pouair Fort

Paris Gate

Bannier Gate

Regnard Gate

Twelve Stones Fort

from Blois →

Fort St. Laurent

Tourelles

Fort des Augustins

St. Privé Fort

Fort St. Jean Le Blanc

6

VICTORY BELLS ARE RUNG

THEY SLEPT IN THE FIELDS that first night. Joan refused to remove her armor and found that sleep would not come easy. When she awoke, she was bruised all over and more weary, almost, than when she lay down. But it was not all due to physical reasons only. She was worried, but not, as anyone else in her place would have been, about the responsibility that now rested on her shoulders, that for more than three thousand human beings and, beyond that, for the result of the operation.

She knew no doubts about her mission. She was worried because she had the intuitive feeling that her commanders had secrets before her.

She had given orders to proceed all the way on the right side of the river Loire. Several commanders, including the experienced and self-assured Marshal Saint-Sévère, had been for the left side. The right side, they maintained, was the more dangerous one. Most of the English fortifications—in fact, a whole string of the forts which rimmed the city—were on that side and, therefore, also the main part of their troops. A headlong attack against these forces was the last thing that appeared to be desirable when the only object of the French was to get their food-transport into the city. According to all the rules of warfare they were right, and yet Joan insisted loudly on having it her way, which, as she said, was what her Voices had told her.

The commanders gave in, but they gave in as one gives in to a fretful child. There was much shrugging of shoulders, and on some faces she thought she could detect a half-hidden amusement. They seemed to think that while it was good to have her with them as a kind of divine promise of victory, the actual planning should be done by the commanders, experienced in warfare, and not by a young peasant girl.

Joan was worried.

Mass was said again on Thursday morning, a strange Mass in the open field, with the morning mist rising. Then the march began again. Suddenly Joan saw that the

Loire was flowing on the wrong side—to the left of her—and now she knew: she had been tricked.

There was Orléans. She could clearly see its walls and towers as well as the fortifications of the English, but all of them were on the other side of the large river.

White with anger, she spurred her horse up to the commanders.

"You have acted against my orders!"

They smiled; they pleaded with her. Their excuse was that news had come from Dunois, the heroic defender of Orléans, that he much preferred this way and that he would send them pontoons and other boats to get the food-transport across.

The Maid asked sharply: "And where are they?"

The faces of the commanders fell. No pontoon, not a single boat, was in sight.

"We couldn't foresee that", Marshal Saint-Sévère stammered.

"You couldn't—but God could", was the stony answer.

Somebody shouted: "A boat is coming—but only one."

It was Dunois himself, with a few of his officers. They came ashore, looking as embarrassed as Joan's commanders. Dunois, a fine figure of a man—tall, broad-shouldered, with a handsome, clean-cut face—walked straight up to Marshal Saint-Sévère.

But before he reached him, an imperious young voice exclaimed: "Are you the commander of Orléans?"

He turned toward it, and now only he recognized in

the tiny armored figure the Maid of whom he had heard so much within the last weeks. His intelligent, brown eyes tried to size her up, but at the same time he was bowing courteously.

"I am—and I am very glad about your arrival."

Joan was in no mood for compliments. "Is it you who advised them to bring me here by this bank of the river, instead of sending me straight to where Talbot and the English are? The provisions could be within the walls now, if my orders had been followed."

Dunois gulped. He was the son of the Duke of Orléans, the finest blade in France, the one French commander who had never been beaten by the enemy. No one, for many years, had dared to talk to him like this. But he controlled himself. "I and others wiser than myself have given this advice, believing it to be the best and wisest", he said gently.

"In the Name of God," Joan exploded, "the counsel of our Lord is wiser and better than yours. You thought to deceive me, but you only managed to deceive yourselves, for I bring you the finest help ever received by knight or city, since it is the help of the King of Heaven. And not for love of me has he sent it, but God himself has listened to the prayer of Saint Louis and is moved to pity for the town of Orléans."

Dunois crossed himself. Then he smiled ruefully. "The mistake is made", he admitted. "I have all the boats ready for the transport of the provisions, but they are not numerous enough to carry the troops as well. Worse still,

I cannot get them upstream—not with this wind blowing. It is most unfortunate."

For the first time he saw something of the real Joan. She looked past him into space, her face tense and pale. Was she praying? She certainly seemed to have become utterly unaware of anybody and anything around her. Then she sighed deeply as if she were awaking from sleep. Her face resumed its usual active and vivacious expression, and she said in a completely matter-of-fact voice: "We must wait. The wind will change soon."

"It's an east wind", Dunois said hesitantly. "It only started a few hours ago, and it usually lasts for days."

"You must learn to believe me", Joan replied.

"Give him time", La Hire said. "Name of God, he'll learn it. By my stick, it's not an easy thing to take for granted. I had to learn it myself and, by my stick, even I sometimes flop like a . . . like a . . ."

" 'Sceptic' is the word you're looking for, captain", Marshal Gilles de Rais put in smoothly.

"Not at all", La Hire told him gruffly. "I was looking for something quite different, and, believe me, I found it, but I mustn't say it." He grinned good-naturedly at Joan, and the Maid smiled back and gave him a friendly pat on his armored back.

"Don't tell me you have given up swearing?" Dunois asked, wide-eyed. "If the Maid has got you to do *that*, I'll gladly believe anything."

"Look", Gilles de Rais shouted. His trembling finger

pointed to the flags, standards, and banners carried by the group of knights behind the commanders. They were fluttering in the wind—*toward the east.*

"The wind has changed." La Hire's rough voice was unsteady.

"The hand of God", Dunois stammered. He was shaken to the core.

"Yes, yes, of course", Joan said impatiently. "Now let's get those boats up straight away."

"I will go and get them", Dunois said eagerly. Despite his heavy armor he ran back to his boat like a boy. Half an hour later the transports were moving to provide the starving city with enough meat and flour for weeks. Soon the work was in full swing.

There was no sign of interference on the part of the enemy, but Dunois, returning, warned once more that his boats could not ferry the army over. "The English cannot possibly let it happen; they're bound to attack, and, when they do, they'll find at least some of the troops helpless in the middle of the river and some on the right and some on the left bank. Nothing could suit them better than to defeat our forces piecemeal. Also, I'd like to have a few days to put fresh strength into the bodies of my own men in the city—and into their minds too."

"You've got all the stuff you need for their bodies," La Hire said, "but what are you going to do about their minds?"

Dunois looked at Joan. "I herewith invite the Maid to

enter the city of Orléans", he said solemnly. "I can think of nothing more apt to raise the courage and strength of the defenders."

Joan frowned. Her Voices had said nothing about that, and she did not want to leave her army. Saint-Sévère and his commanders agreed with Dunois and pleaded with her to accept the invitation.

"I will do it", she said reluctantly. "Let the army return to Blois without engaging the enemy. There must be no engagement without my being there. Return to Orléans as soon as you can, but this time on the right bank! When you come, we shall make a sortie."

"Magnificent", Dunois said, beaming.

"It is not fit that the Maid should come without a suitable retinue", La Hire said suddenly. "I'll come, too— and a few of my men. A dozen will do."

"I'm coming with you, too", cried Florent d'Illiers, one of the younger commanders.

Dunois agreed to take five or six hundred men into Orléans beside the Maid, and now Joan was satisfied.

As soon as night approached, the French army began to withdraw. In the beleaguered city the bells of all the churches began to toll, for once not to announce danger, but joy.

Thousands of citizens came streaming out into the streets, carrying torches and lanterns.

They saw the Maid, riding on a white charger and carrying her standard, with Dunois, jubilant and smiling beside her, and followed by La Hire, Florent d'Illiers, d'Aulon, little Louis de Contes, heralds and trumpeters, and behind them two hundred heavily armored knights with their retinues—six hundred men in all.

And still the bells were tolling.

They felt as if the gates of Heaven had opened to send them help. The Maid—the mysterious creature about whom they had been whispering and talking and debating for weeks on end, whom many had thought did not really exist at all except in the minds of a few clever people trying to raise false hopes and in the minds of those who were ready to believe anything—had come. Here she was in person, looking like an angel in shining armor, Saint Michael in the guise of a young girl, proud and defiant and carrying a standard with the picture of Christ on it. Victory was entering Orléans.

They pressed all around her. They tried to touch her, to touch her standard and her horse. In the general upheaval somebody's torch came too near the white standard and set it ablaze. A cry of horror and dismay went up.

Joan spurred her horse, swung the banner around, and herself extinguished the flame before anyone else could come to her help.

The crowd roared with enthusiasm.

Only when the cavalcade had crossed the entire city from east to west did Joan ask to be taken to her quarters. Dunois had arranged for her to stay at the house of the treasurer of the Duke of Orléans.

There they helped her out of her heavy armor. A

meal was ready for her, but all she would have was again a cup with a little wine mixed with water and a few small pieces of bread, which she dipped into the cup.

Standing beside Dunois, La Hire muttered: "Thank God for that."

"What do you mean?" Dunois asked him in a low voice.

"She's eating something", La Hire whispered. "She didn't have a thing all day and . . ."

"Did you think she was going to faint?"

"No. I thought maybe she never eats at all. But she is human . . . thank God, she is human."

She was human. There were some who still did not believe in her mission. One of them was the Sieur Jean de Gamache, Dunois' own standard-bearer, huge and valiant, but vain. There was a council of war the next day about what was to be done until the French army returned from Blois. La Hire and Florent d'Illiers were all for plaguing the English, Jean de Gamache and a few others were opposed to it, Dunois was undecided.

The Maid, as usual, was for fighting.

Jean de Gamache crashed his fist on the table. "This is a matter to be decided by experienced commanders", he snapped.

"I am the commander", the Maid said sternly.

Jean de Gamache looked at Dunois, who remained silent. This was too much. "Sirs," he said in a thick voice, "if you prefer to take the advice of a lowly country wench rather than that of a knight of my rank, I will no longer protest." He furled his banner and gave it back to Dunois. "I'll be nothing but a humble squire from now on, but I prefer a nobleman as my master and not a woman who is worth nothing."

Joan's eyes were flashing, and Dunois had to exercise all his tact and skill to bring about some sort of a reconciliation.

La Hire was permitted to make a casual attack. He took the English by surprise and secured a few minor advantages in the sector before Saint Pouair. Dunois was able to tell Joan that the herald she had sent to the English was still alive, though a prisoner, but that the English had threatened to have him put to death. "I shall send them a message, too," he added, "and I shall have it shot into one of their forts with an arrow. I'll tell them that if they kill him, I'll have every English prisoner killed."

Joan agreed to that, but she insisted on dictating still another letter to the commander of the English troops, asking them to raise the siege and withdraw to England. When she received no answer, she rode up to the English fortifications where they were strongest, at the Tourelles fort. She could see one of the English commanders on the wall, and someone in her retinue told her that it was Sir William Glasdale.

"Glasdale, Glasdale," she shouted, "in the Name of God, give yourselves up and save your lives."

Sir William roared with laughter. "Go home, cowgirl", he shouted back. "Mind your cows." He added a few strongly worded insults, and other English soldiers joined in.

"Liars", Joan answered. She turned her horse and rode back. No one even troubled to shoot at her. The enemy was not taking her seriously.

Altogether, the English, accustomed as they were to winning against the old-fashioned fighting tactics of the French, displayed supreme indifference to the Maid.

Dunois decided to go to Blois in person and lead the march of the army toward Orléans. The English did not stop him from slipping through their lines. During his absence the Maid was in supreme command of the city, with La Hire as her subcommander.

Three days later, on May 3, the French army came, reinforced, on Dunois' request, by the garrisons of Gien, Montargis, Chateau Reynard, and Chateaudun. They marched on the right side of the river, just as Joan had ordered.

Sentries high up on the church towers of Saint Pierre Empont and Saint Paul hastily descended and reported the approach of a forest of lances and banners. The excitement in Orléans was indescribable.

Joan, with La Hire and five hundred men, rode out of the city to meet Dunois and his men. Now, by all the rules of war, was the moment for the English to attack. They did not. They did not even attack the Maid with her small contingent when she passed by their fortifications. It was as if they had been struck by blindness, and some people in Orléans began to murmur that the Maid had cast a spell on them.

Dunois had news. Sir John Fastolf, the English commander who had won the "battle of the herrings", was on his way once more with a convoy of foodstuffs for the English and would arrive in a day or so.

"In God's name," Joan said hotly, "I order you to let me know as soon as he is in sight. If he passes without my knowledge, I will have your head off."

There was dead silence. "I shall certainly let you know", Dunois said, swallowing hard.

Joan went to bed early that day. She had been out and about since dawn and was dog-tired.

D'Aulon, keeping the watch in front of her door as usual, thought he could hear the sound of distant guns, but he was not sure.

Suddenly the door opened and Joan appeared, white as chalk and trembling with excitement. "My Voices", she cried. "Why didn't you wake me? They're fighting. They're fighting without me, and they'll lose because I'm not with them."

Friar Pasquerel came running.

"French blood is flowing", Joan wailed. "My arms— my armor."

Little Louis de Contes appeared, rubbing the sleep from his eyes.

"My horse", Joan shouted at him.

Never was she armed so quickly, and yet it was not quick enough for her. She raced down the stairs, where

Louis de Contes had her horse ready. "My standard", she cried. "Get it at once!"

D'Aulon, still in the upper floor of the house, took it and threw it out of the window. She caught it and at the same moment spurred her horse. She galloped through the streets, and sparks flew as her horse's hooves struck the pavement.

Louis de Contes followed as quickly as he could, and d'Aulon raced after them as soon as he had put on his own armor. He caught up with her at the Burgundian Gate. There before them was the battle, and the French were having the worst of it. Dunois had attacked, but the English were ready for him this time. The first fugitives came streaming back.

Joan raised her banner and pointed to Fort Saint-Loup. "Turn around, Frenchmen", she cried. "*There* is the enemy." She pressed on, without looking to see whether they would follow her or not. They did. . . .

Dunois himself was in the thick of fighting, furious and ashamed that the battle was going so badly. It was intolerable to think that he would have to tell the Maid about a French defeat. But there was no way of piercing the iron lines of the Godons, who fought as cold-bloodedly as ever and would not give way a yard.

"Back", gasped Jean de Gamache beside him. "Back, my lord, or you'll be cut off. The right wing is giving way all the time."

Dunois was looking at his trumpeter. Just as he was going to give the signal for retreat, another trumpet behind him blew the call for advance. Turning in his saddle, Dunois saw the Maid galloping into the battle. Little Louis de Contes was at her side, with a trumpet raised to his lips and blowing away as hard as he could.

A shout of a thousand voices went up. Regular troops, citizens of Orléans, everybody rushed forward.

All sorts of stories had been told about the Maid in the English camp. However much they jeered and made fun of her, there were many who thought she might well be a witch or a demon. What they saw now seemed to confirm it. How else could it be explained that a mere girl was riding straight at them, swinging her banner? How else could it be explained that the same French, who only just were beginning to flee, now rallied and came on with a rush? No doubt, the Maid was a demon. Or . . . or . . . was she a saint? Did the saints fight for France?

They wavered. The French saw that they wavered and yelled with triumph. "God and the Maid", they yelled.

"God and the Maid", roared Dunois and rode forward.

The English lines broke. White with anger, their commander gave the order to retire into the fort, but he gave it too late. The French were right in their lines, hacking and lunging, and a mixed stream of English and French poured into Fort Saint-Loup.

Smoke began to pour from its woodwork.

Dunois himself was in the fort now, and his heavy

sword crashed through enemy helmets as if they were made of straw.

The Maid, however, did not enter the fort. She stopped and looked westward, toward the main English line of fortifications. There was the English High Command; there was Talbot. And Talbot would see Fort Saint-Loup burning. He would make a sortie.

She rode over to the right wing. It had rallied too, ashamed of its flight, and she ordered the men to follow her. They did, all six hundred of them, and she led them westward and up the slopes of a hill.

"Halt", she commanded. "Dig in your pikes."

A long line of men was coming up from the west— Talbot's men. Just as she thought, they had made a sortie to come to the rescue of Fort Saint-Loup. But they too saw that the way there was no longer free, that the French had anticipated their movement. Perhaps the attack against Fort Saint-Loup was only a feint? Perhaps it had been only a mock attack, and the French were laying a trap for them?

Joan saw the long line coming to a standstill at half a mile distance; then it began to move again . . . backward. She smiled grimly. Her men cheered. She raised herself in the saddle. "We're going back", she said, but when she arrived at Fort Saint-Loup the battle was over. The fort was burning, the English had withdrawn in haste, and Dunois came up to her, sword in hand. "You have won the battle that I lost", he said. "I crave your pardon most humbly. And if you want my head—as you said you would if I attacked without you—here it is, and here is my sword."

She smiled at him. "I knew you would try to deceive me", she said. "It is forgiven."

"We have killed half the garrison of Saint-Loup", Dunois told her.

To his surprise, Joan looked deeply distressed. "It is very terrible", she said. "So many of them died without confession—so many of them. And on the eve of Ascension Day, too." Tears were trickling down her cheeks. She wiped them off with her mailed glove. "All prisoners are to be treated well", she ordered. "And all men-at-arms must go and confess their sins. Then they will give thanks to God for this victory."

"All the troops?" Dunois could not help asking. "That will be hard work for the priests", he added a little lamely.

"All the troops", she affirmed. "If my order is not carried out, I shall leave Orléans and the army. And there will be no plundering of the Church of Saint-Loup. I rely on you this time, Commander Dunois."

Half an hour later all the church bells of Orléans began to ring again for the first victory of the Maid.

7

THE BANNER WAVERS

THERE WAS NO FIGHTING on Ascension Day. The entire French army went to confession, Mass, and Holy Communion instead.

But a war council took place in the town hall, with the Sieur de Gaucourt, governor of the city of Orléans, presiding. The Maid was invited—but a couple of hours later than the others. The leaders of war wanted to make their plans without her untimely interference. As the Sieur de Gaucourt put it jovially, the Maid was no doubt sent by God to bolster up the morale of the troops. In that capacity she was a most welcome help, but the planning of strategy and tactics should be done by those who had studied the art of war, not by a young girl of seventeen. Surely that was obvious. . . .

Perhaps it was not quite so obvious to some of the officers who had seen the Maid transforming a battle thoroughly lost into a resounding victory, and only twenty-four hours before, at that. But they too had to wrestle with their vanity as men and military leaders. Besides, the Sieur de Gaucourt was a very powerful man and supported in his views by the great commanders sent to Orléans by the dauphin—the Marshal Saint-Sévère, the Marshal Gilles de Rais, and most of the others.

"By my stick," La Hire grumbled, "it's my opinion that you have the choice between two things: to do as the Maid tells you and win, or to follow your own counsel and get licked as usual." He stretched his long legs under the table. "I always say what I think", he added, quite unnecessarily.

The Sieur de Gaucourt pointed out that the supreme commander of Orléans, the great Dunois, had not been beaten ever and that it was only right that he should lead the army. Surely it would be grossly unfair if all that he had done and risked for France should count for nothing just because the Maid had arrived! Besides, it was he who had taken Fort Saint-Loup and not the Maid.

Dunois, a little overcome by so much praise, bowed

gracefully and . . . gave in. The Sieur de Gaucourt now proceeded to suggest his own plan of attack. It consisted of a strong feint directed at Fort Saint-Laurent, which most likely would make the English send help there from the southern bank of the river. Then the main attack would be made against the reduced English troops in the south.

"The Maid will join us here in due course", de Gaucourt went on. "We shall tell her about the feint, but not about the main attack."

"Why not?" La Hire asked innocently.

"Because", de Gaucourt answered acidly, "her temperament is such that she would contradict just for the sake of contradicting, as women always will."

The Maid, in the meantime, had written a third and last letter to the English, threatening them with complete destruction unless they left France. She had gone once more as near as possible to the English camp and had the letter shot into it with an arrow. Once again the English reacted only with insults, and she retired sadly, but now, she felt, she had done all she could to avert disaster. If war was the only language they understood, war was what they would get. She rode to the town hall.

There she was told about the plan to attack Fort Saint-Laurent in the morning. She listened coldly. "Very well," she said, "now tell me what you have really decided. I can keep far greater secrets than that."

La Hire grinned at the puzzled captains. "Serves you right", he said. "Maybe you'll learn it one of these days."

Dunois, tactful as ever, said gently: "Please do not be angry with us, Joan. We can't tell you everything at once. What the Sieur de Gaucourt has told you is quite true, but we have decided also to cross the river and attack the English in the south. I think it's a very good plan, and we hope you will agree."

"So be it", she said curtly, turned around, and left.

Early on May 6 the French crossed the river on an improvised bridge of boats and barges, hastily put together under the protection of the morning mist. The militia, which had been assigned to make the feint on Fort Saint-Laurent, had insisted in the end on going across to fight on the south bank with the rest of the army.

When the English finally saw them approaching, they evacuated the weak Fort Saint-Jean-le-Blanc and retired to the strong Fort des Augustins, a former monastery.

Soon the French were to see that the evacuation of Saint-Jean-le-Blanc had been a feint. Streaming out of the Fort des Augustins, the English threatened to attack them from the rear. The French began to waver, then to retreat. It was an orderly retreat, and, what is more, Dunois himself commanded it. He was satisfied with having captured another English fort.

Joan was not. "The way to the enemy is this side", she cried, and once more attacked all by herself, banner in hand. La Hire at once turned his horse and followed her. "God and the Maid", he shouted.

He was heard. The French troops turned, looked,
. . . and attacked, instead of withdrawing, with Jean
d'Aulon in the vanguard. The guns of the Fort des
Augustins roared, and huge cannon balls smashed into
the ranks of the attackers. The French were fought to a
standstill, and the English counterattacked furiously. All
around the Maid men fell dead and wounded. La Hire
had sent half a dozen men to the rear to ask for reinforcements, but none would come, and once more the
French began to retire. Many fell into the river and more
often than not were drowned, unable to rise again in
their heavy armor.

Some of the English began to dismantle the bridge
and to fill the boats and barges. Their counterattack now
threatened Orléans itself.

"Back", La Hire gasped. "Back, Joan. There'll be
another day."

But the Maid shook her head. "Now is the time", she
said fiercely.

To his horror La Hire saw her turn again and attack
alone. "Frenchmen," he yelled, "are you going to let the
Maid die?"

Five, ten, twenty, fifty men turned and took up the
shout, and hundreds responded to it. Like a wave rolling
back, they followed into the mist of powder in which
the Maid had vanished. The English, in their hot pursuit, had opened their ranks, and the sudden furious
assault of the French took them by surprise. More than
two hundred of them had fallen before the others rallied,

and now the battle was on once more. Every inch of the ground was fought for bitterly.

The banner of the Maid was still visible. La Hire had reached her and warded off one enemy stroke after the other.

In the middle of the tumult the Maid coolly ordered d'Aulon to collect as many men as he could and to take the English in the rear.

D'Aulon obeyed, but the English commander saw the danger in time and ordered the retreat behind the walls of the Augustinian fort.

"Ladders", the Maid shouted. "Ladders, and the fort is ours."

Inside the city the women and the old people were kneeling in the churches, praying for the Maid, for victory, for their men out there.

From afar they could hear the noise of the fighting, swelling, ebbing, swelling again. The gunfire ceased. What did it mean?

They went on praying. After what seemed to be an eternity, a man in full armor came clanking into the cathedral. "Give your thanks to God for the Maid", he cried. "We have taken the Augustinian fort."

The population was still pressing around the Maid and her horse, throwing flowers at her, praising her to the sky, kissing her armored feet and mailed hands, when the captains and commanders were planning again. They had taken three English forts and killed more Godons than in the seven months before the Maid arrived. The Maid had been of the greatest help, but the French army had suffered serious losses, and the English still outnumbered them considerably. In the circumstances, was it not better to do no more fighting for a while and wait until reinforcements had come in from the dauphin's headquarters? Surely he would agree to that and make it possible, now that they something to show for their efforts? There was no danger that the English would launch a general attack when they had not done so at a time when their whole string of forts had been intact. Besides, the town was much better off for food. Further convoys could come in from the south without much danger from interference, now that Fort Saint-Jean-le-Blanc, Fort Saint-Loup, and the Augustinian fort were out of the way. . . .

When the Maid came, they told her they had decided not to fight at present—certainly not tomorrow.

Joan glared at them. "You have been with your council, and I have been with mine. Believe me, my council will hold good and will be accomplished; yours will come to nothing."

Before she went to bed she told her confessor, Friar Pasquerel: "Reverend Friar, I must ask you to get up still earlier than usual tomorrow morning. You must be with me all the time, for it will be a dangerous day. I shall get wounded here . . ."—and she pointed to her breast—"and you must be there to hear my last confession if the wound should prove to be fatal."

The commanders, still assembled, were angry and ill at ease. It seemed as if the Maid deliberately turned aside every idea and every decision except her own, and no one could say what she was up to this time. "I don't mind it when she takes the enemy by surprise," the Marshal Saint-Sévère said ruefully, "but she will insist on surprising us as well."

"This girl", La Hire declared, "is the most courageous man I ever saw."

"Of course, of course." The Sieur de Gaucourt raised his hands. "No one here is doubting her courage, or the most singular influence she seems to have on the troops. Perhaps she really possesses supernatural forces. . . ."

"If she does," Florent d'Illiers interposed quickly, "then these forces are coming from God and the saints."

"Another point I will gladly concede", de Gaucourt replied. "But the fact is that she alone possesses them. Perhaps she never gets tired. Ordinary soldiers do, though, and our men have been driven to the utmost effort. They need a rest. Besides, the Maid, notwithstanding all her wonderful qualities, takes too many risks."

"They were worth it, weren't they?" La Hire barked.

"They were in the past. Who can tell whether her luck will hold?"

"Luck?" La Hire jumped to his feet. "Call it inspired generalship! What other word could there be for the last attack of hers, when we all thought the battle was lost

and she alone saw that the English had loosened their
ranks? And her order, as soon as we had conquered the
Augustinian fort, to turn the cannons round and start
firing at the Tourelles fort?"

"The fighting qualities of the Maid are beyond dis-
pute," Saint-Sévère said indulgently, "but there is no
doubt also that she is extremely fond of taking the grav-
est risks. It is our duty to see to it that our troops will not
be exposed to more danger than necessary."

"You don't understand her at all", La Hire said gruffly.
"You always complain that she's making her own decisions, but it's she who ought to make the decisions, and
thank God she does. It's not a case of her hampering
your war effort; it's you who's hampering hers."

"Steady, La Hire, steady", Dunois said affably. "There's
truth in everything that was said here—including what
you said—but there's no need to be rude."

"If it's rude to be for fighting when the English are at
the gates, I'll gladly be rude."

Dunois smiled at the others. "We are all for fighting,"
he said, "every one of us, but prudence is as necessary in
war as courage. We have agreed that there shall be no
fighting tomorrow. Let's leave it at that for the time
being and meet again tomorrow evening."

"I wonder what the Maid will do", La Hire said with
a smirk.

Sieur de Gaucourt pressed his lips together. "I happen
to be the governor of this city," he said acidly, "and I'll
see to it that she will not interfere with the decision of

the council. I shall give orders to keep all the gates closed."

La Hire grinned at him. "Now I *really* wonder. . . ." he said.

Commander Vitry, in charge of the Burgundian Gate, rubbed his eyes when he saw the forces advancing on it, not from outside, but from within. He remembered his orders and shouted at them: "No one leaves the city." He posted his fifty men in such a way that they formed a living wall.

A number of knights arrived and demanded the keys. He refused steadfastly. Then the Maid rode up, banner in hand. "Open up."

Commander Vitry tried to reason with her. In the meantime he dispatched a messenger on horseback to fetch the Sieur de Gaucourt. He and fifty soldiers against what seemed to be a small army, and commanded by the Maid in person! The odds were not much to his liking.

The soldiers—and with them quite a number of armed militia—began to become uneasy. A shout went up for axes and another for a rope to hang him. But the worst was the face of the Maid, white, with big, blazing eyes. "I will not have Frenchmen fighting Frenchmen", the Maid shouted to her men. "Use your axes against the small door over there; demolish part of the wall. Fight only if this officer's men try to interfere with you."

Vitry shrugged his shoulders. "I'll give you the key", he said dejectedly. "Here, take it." Joan smiled and gave a sign to little Louis de Contes, who took the key eagerly and opened the gate. The soldiers began to pour out into the open.

When the Sieur de Gaucourt arrived, breathless and angry, both regular troops and armed militia were still streaming out of the gate. The Maid was gone.

"Next time," Vitry told him, "you'd better put an archangel in charge here. Maybe he can stop the Maid. I certainly can't."

For one wild moment the Sieur de Gaucourt seriously considered having the gate closed again and leaving the Maid, with those who had followed her, outside to be massacred by the English. But then he overcame his temper. The Maid was the symbol of victory for the army and for the citizens of Orléans. They would tear him to pieces if he left her in the lurch. Silently he turned his horse and rode back to report the matter to Dunois.

To his surprise, Dunois gave a hearty laugh. "I expected something of the kind", he said. "And La Hire was sure of it. Of course we can't leave her out there. Give the signs for general alarm. The earlier we reach her the better. God alone knows what she's up to. What did you do with Vitry?"

"Nothing. If *we* can't stop her, how can I expect him to do it? I looked back after a while and there he was, slipping out of the gate himself."

Dunois grinned and began to give orders right and left. "It's sheer madness", he said to La Hire, when they were riding to the Burgundian Gate themselves, half an hour later. "We have no plan, and no target, nothing."

"The Maid is out there", La Hire answered calmly. "That's good enough for me."

But even he looked worried when they saw that the Maid had made her troops form a semicircle around the Tourelles Fort. Here the English had the strongest of their garrisons, commanded by Sir William Glasdale, Talbot's most trusted commander, a rough soldier who had sworn to catch the Maid and have her burned to death as a witch.

Tourelles was far stronger than the Augustinian fort, to say nothing of the others.

"They'll do anything to beat her back", Dunois said. "They can't afford to lose the Tourelles. If they do, the whole siege would have to be broken off."

"That's why she chose to attack it", La Hire said.

Dunois nodded. "Without waiting for us, too", he said. "With fewer than a thousand men."

"Perhaps you will believe me now", said someone just behind him. "Didn't I tell you she couldn't be trusted with the command? Why, the woman is mad."

Turning, Dunois recognized Jean de Gamache.

"If the Maid is mad," La Hire said, "I'd hate to be normal." But in the next moment he gave a gasp. The Maid herself was attacking the redoubt on the land side of the fort. She had jumped off her horse and pointed her banner toward the wall. Ladders were being brought into position.

"Oh, no", La Hire cried. "She mustn't do that. They'll get her!"

But she was already climbing up the ladder, banner in hand.

La Hire spurred his horse and rode toward the redoubt as fast as he could.

"The English can't afford to lose the Tourelles," Dunois said, "but we can't afford to lose the Maid. La Hire is right. Forward!"

They broke down on the Tourelles in a mass assault.

A dozen ladders were put in position by now, all swarming with armored men. Higher and higher went the banner of the Maid, its white silk lit up by the morning sun.

Then it happened. The sacred emblem seemed to gain a life of its own. It swung round and began not to fall but to sink, like a small white cloud. And the tiny figure who had carried it was falling, falling headlong into the moat.

A howl of horror went up in the French ranks. "The Maid . . . the Maid is dead."

Sir William Glasdale was standing high up on the redoubt. "That's it", he said coolly. "Ready for the sortie, Poynings? Right. Open the gate! Out with you, my men! And you, Ludlow and Hall and Blackwell, see if the damned witch is dead. If she isn't, catch her. Fifty pieces of gold for her, dead or alive."

The ironclad gate clanked open, and the English, in tight formation, broke into the ranks of the French. The double surprise of the fall of the Maid and the sortie of the English was too much. The French wavered and fell back—but not all of them, not La Hire, who gave young Lord Poynings the fight of his life and roared to his men to stem the English advance, and not another commander who, with a handful of men, jumped into the moat and carried the Maid out. They shielded her with their own bodies, fighting like madmen.

From above came Sir William Glasdale's voice. "What's the matter? Haven't you got her yet?"

They had not. Ludlow fell under the stroke of a huge mace, Hall was pushed into the moat, and Blackwell tried in vain to surround the French commander and his few men who managed to retire still farther with their precious burden, until they had reached safety.

Opening her eyes, Joan saw the face of Jean de Gamache bent over her. "You?" she said in a low voice.

"I did you wrong", he said. "You're a great commander. Please forgive me. I'll try to make up for what I said."

She smiled at him. Then she winced, and her hand went up to her breast. An arrow stuck there, the arrow of a crossbowman. It had pierced her chain mail and gone deeply into the flesh.

La Hire rushed up, and soon afterward Dunois himself. They found her crying and asking for her confessor. Friar Pasquerel was sent for and came up in a hurry. Everybody else stepped back.

The commanders glanced at each other. They had

never seen her like this before. The imperious Maid, the inspired commander of men, was transformed into a weeping girl. Perhaps this was the end?

Just out of earshot they watched Friar Pasquerel giving her absolution. A moment later he came up to them. "You may approach now", he said. "She wants you to."

They did. The Maid was no longer crying. She smiled at them. "I have been comforted", she said. "The soul is whole. Now for the body." With a firm hand she seized the arrow sticking in her flesh and pulled it out as if it were a mere splinter. Her blood flowed freely.

Somebody had the sense to apply a dressing drenched in olive oil and put a bandage on top of it.

"You shouldn't be here", she said to Dunois. "How is the battle going?"

"Not too well", Dunois told her frankly. "Talbot has sent reinforcements, and I have arranged for a slow withdrawal."

"No withdrawal", she cried. "No withdrawal."

"What must be must be, Joan", Dunois said gently. "And the English are not pressing the pursuit. There has been no more gunfire for quite a little while either."

She frowned. "I don't know", she said in a voice full of grief. "I don't know yet. I must . . . get up."

"No, don't", Dunois pleaded. "We shall have you carried back into the city. Just wave from time to time to the soldiers so that they see that you are still alive. It will give them fresh confidence, and they'll need it—another day."

"I must get up", she repeated dully, and at once she

began to struggle to her feet. La Hire tried to help her, but she was up before he could touch her. "My banner", she said. "Where is my banner?"

"Here it is", said Jean de Gamache, handing it to her.

"I too have misjudged you", she said. "You are a good man. Keep it until I return. Let the troops rest and have some food. I shall be back soon."

She walked away, slowly but erect and without looking back.

Dunois shook his head. "She drew out the arrow herself", he said. "Here it is—the wound went deep. And she rose without help and there she walks. What is this girl made of?"

"God knows." Jean de Gamache looked at the banner in his hands. "Remember how I refused to go on carrying your banner, my Lord Dunois, because of her? And now she's given me her own, and it makes me feel more proud than any honor ever accorded to me. Where is she going?"

"Into the vineyard over there."

They could see her, half-hidden by the vines, a tiny figure.

"She's down on her knees", Jean de Gamache cried. "She's fainting." He made a move to follow her, but La Hire held him back.

"She's not fainting", he said quietly. "She's praying."

She came back after a quarter of an hour. Her steps were firm now, and her eyes were shining. "My horse", she said. "My banner. Follow me. The day is ours."

"But, Joan . . ." Dunois stammered. "Those who love me, follow me", she said, and she mounted her horse without help.

The defenders of the redoubt could not believe their eyes when the French attacked again. Cold fear gripped them when they saw in the very midst of the first rank the Maid, swinging her banner.

They had seen her fall from the ladder into the moat. They knew she had been struck by an arrow from an English crossbow—and here she was, on horseback, banner and all.

"She *is* a witch."

"She can't be human."

"We can't fight demons. . . ."

An old soldier who was said to have "second sight" cried that the air was full of Power and that he could see huge riders on winged horses galloping in the sky just above the Maid.

"Don't talk such rot", Sir William Glasdale shouted. "Shoot, you superstitious devils, shoot."

They obeyed, but their shooting was nervous and haphazard, and before their commander could rally them, the French were upon them.

Through the din of the fighting came the voice of the Maid, loud and clear: "Glasdale . . . Glasdale . . . surrender to the King of Heaven. I feel pity for your soul and for the souls of your people."

Sir William cursed roundly. His men were getting the

worst of it, and he had to act quickly. The redoubt could no longer be held. The thing to do was to retire across the wooden bridge that combined the redoubt with the main fort, and he gave orders accordingly.

His soldiers were only too glad to obey. They streamed back in disorder, followed by their officers.

Joan gave a sign with her banner, the sign for the French guns to shoot in the direction she pointed. D'Aulon was in charge of them.

The very first shot tore a hole into the bridge. The next three, fired as a salvo, smashed a group of English officers to pulp. Among them was Glasdale himself.

Over their mangled bodies the French pursued the defenders into the fort. A last, furious struggle around the main gate, and then the attackers streamed into Les Tourelles.

8

MASS COMES FIRST

T HE ENGLISH WAR COUNCIL was assembled, safe at
least for the moment in the strong fort of Saint-
Laurent.

"Gentlemen," said General Sir John Talbot, "the loss
of the Tourelles fort is decisive for our position. Without
reinforcements we cannot keep up the siege any longer."
He looked at Colonel Scales, who, apart from other
duties, served as chief of intelligence. Scales shrugged his
shoulders. "His Grace the Duke of Bedford is trying to

raise fresh levies, but it will be months before they can be here."

There was silence.

Fastolf, an experienced old soldier, gave a harsh laugh. "Beaten", he said. "Beaten by a seventeen-year-old girl. There's nothing like it in military history. So far, every woman who was idiotic enough to assume military command was beaten soundly. Queen Hophra of the Massagetes was beaten by Cyrus. Cleopatra was beaten by Octavian, our own Boadicea by Caesar. What is the world coming to, I'd like to know!"

"I am most obliged to Colonel Fastolf for his lecture on matters historical", Talbot remarked drily. "But what matters here is a quick decision on the basis of facts, however regrettable. I have no doubt at all that this Hophra or Cleopatra of ours will be beaten too in the end. I cannot imagine His Grace leaving France if that French sorceress should write him another of her famous letters. Neither can I visualize England bowing to the whims of a peasant girl from Lorraine. But for the time being, gentlemen, there is not much more we can do here."

"Sorceress", repeated Scales thoughtfully. "Perhaps that is the explanation for friend Fastolf. It certainly is the explanation for many of our men. We're beaten by sorcery."

"I've heard them say so," Fastolf nodded, "and it didn't do their morale any good. But there are some who say that the girl is a saint and that it is impossible to fight a saint, and that is very considerably worse.

"I never heard of a saint fighting against England", Talbot said stiffly.

"With all due respect, Sir John, you've heard of one now", Fastolf dared to say.

Talbot glared at him. "If I didn't know you for a valiant enough soldier, colonel, I'd say you're afraid of an armed girl."

Fastolf touched his sword hilt. "No one's going to accuse me of fear, general", he glowered.

"The girl is a sorceress", Scales insisted. "She must be. Bill Thompson is absolutely certain his arrow went right through her heart, and yet she was back in the battle an hour or two later, shouting and yelling and brandishing that banner of hers. The devil looks after his own, they say. And now she even manages to sow dissension right here in the council of war. A damned witch, that's all she is."

"I shall report to His Grace about that possibility", Sir John Talbot said, with a pale smile. "In the meantime there is the fact that in the course of a week she has cost us four forts and more than three thousand men in dead and wounded. Sir William Glasdale is dead, and so is Lord Poynings. Gentlemen, there are only two choices open to us: either we launch an all-out attack against the city, witch or no witch—an attack of desperation, we might say—or else we must withdraw to safe territory, that is to say, to the headquarters of His Grace. Mind you, we're not likely to be received with open arms. Which is it going to be? Your opinions, gentlemen, please."

General alarm was beaten and blown in the city of Orléans on the morning of Sunday, May 8. The watchmen on towers and turrets had seen the English troops pouring out of all the forts still in their possession. They were forming up in two bodies in the east and north.

The French army assembled and was drawn up in battle order.

Despite the pleadings of the physicians Joan insisted on putting on armor—light armor, at least, without the heavy cuirass.

"If you remain in bed, we can guarantee that you will be quite well in two weeks' time", Doctor Melun told her. "If you rise and go out, we can guarantee nothing."

Her answer was that she shouted for her horse and her banner.

Time and again soldiers in the streets asked her whether they would be allowed to fight today, on Sunday.

"Mass comes first", she replied.

At the Burgundian Gate she asked for two altars to be erected in full sight of the enemy. Two Masses were to be said.

"What if the Godons attack us now?" La Hire murmured.

"They won't dare," Dunois whispered back, "and if they do, God will never give them victory."

But many French knights and their men were turning toward the enemy front.

The Maid raised her hand. "Stay", she commanded. "It is the will of God that you should observe his holy day. We shall not attack. We shall only defend ourselves, if necessary."

At a distance of less than five hundred yards the English were looking on, thousands of them—a compact, armored mass, topped by the sharp blades of halberds and pikes.

"Mass", Scales said. "They're saying Mass, and the witch is with them. I can see her and her banner. Now is this blasphemy, or . . ."

". . . or is she by any chance not a witch at all?" Fastolf put in.

Talbot said nothing, but he looked as black as a thundercloud. How sure they were of themselves, these Frenchmen, whom he had defeated in every single encounter—before the Maid appeared. How serenely they attended to their divine service, as if no enemy were present within a hundred miles! He turned his horse. "My Lord Suffolk," he said, "you and your men will form the rear guard. Gentlemen, please join your units. We shall move in a quarter of an hour."

On the French side the two Masses went on. At the elevation of the Host, the knights on horseback saluted with their swords; all men on foot went down on their knees, all banners, standards, and pennons were lowered until they almost touched the earth, including the white banner of the Maid, held by Jean d'Aulon. The Maid herself was rapt in prayer.

Holy Communion was distributed, sanctifying the army, transforming it into a sacred wall before the gates of the city.

"*Ite, missa est*", the priest's voice rang out.

As if in answer to his words, a shout came from the nearest watchtower. "They're moving! They're moving!"

The Maid rose and crossed herself. "In what direction?" she asked.

"They're moving away from the city", came the shout. "They're leaving!"

The Maid's young face shone. "In the name of God," she cried, "let them depart, and we will give thanks to God."

La Hire came up to her. "Let me pursue them", he begged.

The Maid glanced at the enemy troops. She saw that the main force was moving fairly quickly in the direction of Jargeau and Meung and that another force, several thousand strong, was following at a much slower pace. Talbot had arranged for a rear guard, it seemed.

"Go," she told La Hire, "but take no more than a thousand men. Even you won't attack with so few. I don't want any bloodshed today, but I do want to know where the English are going.

He nodded and made off.

The Maid took her banner from the hands of Jean d'Aulon and raised it. "Sing," she cried, "sing, all of you. Never again will the English lay siege to Orléans. The city is free. Sing to the glory of God!"

The bonfires in the city were still burning, the good people of Orléans still dancing in the streets, when the Maid left. Her mission here was accomplished. Her next task was elsewhere, and she was not one to waste time.

She left on horseback, but she was no longer wearing armor. Instead she was dressed in a white doublet. White were her long leather boots, white her plumed hat, and white her steed. Every day, from her arrival in Orléans on, she had written to the dauphin, reporting about what happened and, in the same letter, telling him what would happen the next day. Now she was going to meet him in person, to give him the final report. Dunois went with her, La Hire, and d'Aulon, with an escort of a few hundred men. The English troops were still about, and there was always the possibility that they might try to catch their most dangerous enemy with a sudden raid.

"My work has only started", Joan said, when Dunois tried to persuade her to take a rest until her wound was completely healed.

They did not find the dauphin either in Blois or in Tours. He had gone back to Chinon, but dispatch riders reported that he would arrive in Tours very shortly.

As soon as his coming was signaled from the towers of Tours, Joan went out to meet him, taking Dunois, La Hire, d'Aulon, and every man of her retinue with her. Half the population streamed out with them.

At the very gate of the town they saw the cloud of dust formed by the hooves of hundreds of horses. Dunois smiled at the Maid. "This time it's not the English", he said.

"It will be, soon again", she replied. The dauphin rode up with a retinue of the greatest names of France. Many of them had never seen the Maid. All of them were curious how she would behave. One would scarcely expect a peasant girl to know anything about the rules of etiquette at state occasions.

For once, the dauphin's pale, homely face was flushed.

Joan, keeping her banner firmly in her right hand, took off her white hat with the left and bowed deeply and so gracefully that everybody marvelled.

The dauphin stopped his horse alongside hers and embraced and kissed her, a privilege accorded only to royalty. The people shouted, cried, yelled, and roared with enthusiasm.

"Put on your hat," the dauphin said, "and ride into the town at my right side. Tonight the decree of nobility will be handed to you, for you and your entire family."

He himself had ordered the design for her heraldic arms: on a blue field a silver sword supporting a golden crown, between two fleur-de-lis, the royal flower of France.

9

SURPRISED—BY A STAG

T HE ROYAL COURT went to the castle of Loches, and
for some days Joan was the much honored guest of
the dauphin, entertained and acclaimed by all. Even her
old enemies, like the Duke de La Trémoïlle, and her new
ones, like the Sieur de Gaucourt, were treating her with
great courtesy . . . as long as she was present. Behind her
back, however, they were trying their best to convince
the dauphin that the Maid had done everything that
could be expected of her. There was therefore no more
need for her presence at court.

"Orléans has been liberated", the duke said. "The English, said to be invincible, have been beaten. Excellent. But to go on with the war now would be fatal. We cannot expect to be lucky all the time, can we? I have spoken to the commanders. Almost all of them, except that fool La Hire, were much upset by the way in which this girl used to command them about. . . ."

"I have spoken to them myself," the dauphin interrupted, "and they were full of praise for the Maid."

"Because they didn't wish to upset you", the duke replied craftily. "They know how much you're attached to her and her . . . miracles, but to me they speak frankly."

"Because they know that you only want to hear the worst about her, my dear duke." The dauphin could be cuttingly ironical. For years it had been his only weapon.

"Very well, then", the duke said stiffly. "I know she's pressing you and urging you on every day. She wants more laurels for herself. You made her a noblewoman. Maybe she wants to become a duchess. I am certain the English would be quite ready to make a very lenient peace with us now. If you go on with the war, they'll fight to the death and it won't be their death. Troops cost money, Your Highness, and I for once can find no more money. The treasury is empty. In fact, the last army hasn't been paid for yet."

"I still count on your help, my dear duke."

La Trémoïlle gave an angry laugh. "Not a franc," he said, "not a copper coin. If you want to go on with this war, you'll have to find another financial source—if there is any."

Archbishop Regnault de Chartres was all for peace, too. "The duke is right. We might obtain fairly good conditions," he said, "and we must not exaggerate the triumph of the Maid. Neither the English nor the Burgundians will regard themselves as beaten just because the siege of Orléans had to be raised."

"Joan promised to raise that siege," the dauphin said, "and she promised also that she would lead me to Rheims to be crowned there. She has fulfilled the first part of her promise. She should have at least a chance of fulfilling the second. After all, *you* are the Archbishop of Rheims. You would do the crowning. Surely you ought to be all for it. . . ."

"As a priest, Highness, I shall always prefer peace to war. . . ."

"What? With the enemy still on our soil?"

". . . as the Archbishop of Rheims I most certainly would be happy to crown Your Highness in my cathedral, but unfortunately there is little chance that we would get there alive. The way is barred not only by a great number of French cities which are pro-Burgundian and even, I am sorry to say, pro-English, but also by English forces under Sir John Talbot, still holding Jargeau, Meung, and Beaugency. We cannot afford to expose the life of Your Highness to such dangers for the sake of a young woman's bold predictions."

Half an hour later Joan was with the dauphin pleading

for action, immediate action. He listened to her timidly. He did not dare to say yes or no, but tried to please her by nominating the Duke of Alençon as the lieutenant-general of his army under her command. "He will be your right hand."

"I am grateful for such a right hand," Joan said, "as long as I can have the rest of the body, too. Haven't they told you that they want to dissolve the army because there is no money to pay them?"

The dauphin gave a painful smile. "I wish you could let me find the gold I need to pay the men you lead to victory."

"All the gold you need is that of the crown on your head," Joan said, "but you must go out and get it in Rheims."

Shy, suspicious, lacking in courage and determination, the dauphin was no fool. He sensed the statesmanship in Joan's answer. Once he was crowned, he was the King of France for every Frenchman. He could then command their loyalty in every respect instead of having to pay them vast sums for every service they would render to him.

"I will try again", he promised. Perhaps Jacques Coeur, the banker, could help, however degrading it was to resort to mere commoners. But even if he could, nothing could be done without the great nobles who had so many men under their own command.

Negotiations and conferences took place day after day. In the midst of the most important of them all, when the dauphin was closed in with his new confessor, with d'Harcourt, Dunois, the Lord of Trèves, and many others, there was a loud knock at the door. Joan entered and flung herself at the dauphin's feet.

"Noble dauphin, make an end to these long councils and come to Rheims to receive the crown that is yours by right."

The dauphin helped her to her feet. "Did your Voices tell you this?"

"Yes—and they leave me no peace at all."

The dauphin's confessor asked gravely: "What did your Voices say last?"

Joan said in a low voice: "Whenever I am vexed because what I say in the name of God is not believed, I go where I am alone and pray. I tell God how angry I am that those to whom I speak have no faith in my words, and the last time I heard a voice saying, 'Go forward, daughter of God, go, go, go. I will be at your side to help you.'" Her face was radiant now. "I wish I could always hear that", she said in a whisper.

Dunois stepped forward. "Give the word, Sire, and we'll fight."

The dauphin was deeply moved, and yet even now he hesitated.

Joan approached him. All radiance had gone out of her face, now pale and sad. "Gentle dauphin," she said, "see to it that you make good use of me during the next twelve months. I shall not last much longer than that. . . ."

After that she would say no more.

On that day the decision was made to use the services of Jacques Coeur to finance a new campaign. Until a new and much bigger army would be ready and assembled, Joan was given the task to try to conquer the three places on the Loire River still in English hands.

She attacked Jargeau with a force of no more than eighteen hundred men. The militia from Orléans had not arrived yet; neither had the crossbowmen.

Even La Hire swore by his stick that the whole thing was lunacy, and at first he seemed to be right. The English beat off the attack. As usual, Joan rallied her men and prepared the next assault.

Suddenly she said to the young Duke of Alençon beside her: "Gentle Duke, move away from where you are at once." As he looked at her bewildered, she seized his arm and dragged him away.

A few moments later a stone ball from one of the English breech-loaders crashed right on the spot the young duke had just left.

"I promised your sweet wife you would come home safely", Joan smiled. Then she raised her banner and gave the sign for the attack.

This time the French reached the walls of Jargeau. Once again, as at the Tourelles fort, Joan was the first to climb a ladder. Once again, she was thrown into the moat.

"She must have nine lives, like a cat", an English

officer cried, when he saw her jump to her feet almost as soon as she had fallen.

"She's a witch", a tall soldier whispered. "Nothing can hurt her. We're fighting a demon, that's what it is."

The Earl of Suffolk heard it. He was not a superstitious man. Knocking down the soldier with his mailed fist, he shouted: "She's nothing but a mad flea, bred on a dung hill. Down with her and the French."

The "mad flea" retired to a place where the few French cannons were brought into position. The gunners gaped with surprise when Joan herself served one of the guns and directed the fire of the others with smashing success. Guns, surely, were the most intricate weapons. Gunners had been trained for months, and now the Maid outdid them all. Who had taught her the art?

A third attack proved too much for the defenders. Suffolk saw his young brother die. He himself was wounded; half of his men were dead. He parried the first strokes of a young squire, but his arm was weary. He stepped back. "Are you a knight?" he asked his adversary.

"I am Squire Guillaume Regnault from Auvergne."

"The Earl of Suffolk can surrender only to a knight", the Englishman said. "I'll dub you a knight here and now." He touched the young man's shoulder with his sword. "Now you may take the sword that dubbed you", he said. "I am your prisoner."

At that sight the rest of the defenders surrendered.

A little over a week later the French army moved on Meung. Beaugency surrendered as soon as they came in sight. Joan let the garrison withdraw as soon as they had sworn that they would fight no more.

"I hope your spurs are good, Messires", the Maid said cheerfully, when the first enemy troops came in sight.

"Why?" The Duke of Alençon looked worried. "Do you expect us to be beaten, to flee?"

"Oh, no," the Maid smiled, "but you'll need good spurs if you want to catch the fleeing enemy. Our losses will be very small today."

After the fall of Jargeau and the surrender of Beaugency, a fearful quarrel occurred between the two English commanders, Talbot and Fastolf.

Grim old Talbot, who, after all, was the supreme commander, insisted on having it his way, and his way was always to give battle. "They call me the old bull", he said. "Well, I would rather be a bull than a fox like you, Fastolf."

Strangely enough, it was neither a bull nor a fox who would bring about the decision, but a . . . stag.

The English, instead of fighting around Meung, had withdrawn into a near forest, waiting for the French and ready to pounce on them.

Joan, unable to see anything of the enemy, sent out a swarm of scouts. The noise of their horses made a large stag bound off, right into the English lines.

The great majority of the English soldiers were yeomen, men from the country and enthusiastic sportsmen.

They forgot all about the French and, shouting with joy, started a regular hunt. The hunt was still in full swing when the French army broke down on them, surprising them instead of being surprised by them.

In the forest, the forest of Patay, twenty-five hundred Englishmen paid with their blood for a single stag. Sir John Talbot was taken prisoner and, with him, Lord Scales, Sir Thomas Rameston, Lord Hungerford, and many other leaders.

Fastolf alone escaped and fled all the way to the Duke of Bedford's headquarters to report the worst defeat of the English in the entire war. The duke, beside himself with rage, tore the star of the Garter off poor Fastolf's coat.

When Dunois and La Hire, at the end of the battle, looked for the Maid, they found her sitting on a stone, with the head of a dying soldier on her knees. With a quick gesture she cut off the congratulations of her commanders. "Get a priest at once", she said. "This man must make his confession."

The soldier was English.

10

THE DAUPHIN IS CROWNED

Rumors were racing through France. The Maid
was a saint sent by God; no, she was a demon,
trying to bring ruin over the whole country. She was a
subtle, lying wench, out for personal honors, for wealth
and power; she was an instrument of the saints who
wanted to give France back to Frenchmen. The dauphin
was a gullible fool to believe in her; the dauphin was
developing into a true king. The English were as good as
beaten; the English had lost a few skirmishes and with-

drawn, just as the string of the bow is withdrawn before one can shoot a fresh arrow.

What were they to believe, the unfortunate mayors and town councillors, the nobles and bishops, the great, teeming masses of the people?

So many of them had despaired of a dauphin who never went into battle for his right, of whom his own mother had despaired in her time, and who was the tool of this or that ambitious, money-grabbing noble. It was hard to believe that he had changed. What was more, it was dangerous. The English claimed that their king was King of France by right of a perfectly good treaty. The Duke of Burgundy, too, had certain aspirations. And both the English and the Duke of Burgundy had troops at their disposal to enforce their rights and their aspirations.

In the circumstances, could one dare to rely on the recent victories of the dauphin or, rather, on those of the Maid? Could one dare to open the city gates for her and her men and, in doing so, to acknowledge her master, the dauphin? For a hundred years France had been split into warring factions. The Maid was said to have sworn to change all that. But could one believe her? Could one trust her—especially in the face of the rumor that many nobles at the dauphin's own court did not trust her? It was known that they were trying hard to stem her undoubted influence over the weak Dauphin.

Paris certainly was not in the mood to join in what seemed from the banks of the Seine a hopeless adventure.

All that was great and good would surely start in Paris. Could anything good come from the provinces?

Besides, the Duke of Burgundy did not take any chances. He entered Paris with seven hundred heavily armed knights and their retinues, warmly received by the Duke of Bedford, by the learned professors of the world-famous university, and by all the dignitaries of municipal officialdom. There was a solemn Pontifical High Mass in Notre Dame Cathedral, there was a brilliant procession, a magnificent parade. The Rector of the Sorbonne, in full dress and surrounded by the entire teaching body, read out the text of the peace treaty between Charles the Sixth—the dauphin's father and a hopeless lunatic—and the former Duke of Burgundy. Many of the learned people knew only too well that the treaty had been inspired by the crafty, resolute Queen Isabeau and that the king, her husband, did not know what he was doing when he signed the shameful document.

But even in Paris there were voices speaking up for the Maid and the dauphin. At least one friar, a Franciscan, dared to preach about her in the very streets. . . .

The events at Jargeau, Beaugency, and Meung, and especially the battle of the forest of Patay, had given fresh strength to the "Party of the Maid". Jacques Coeur, the banker, made use of his own great credit with foreign banking houses. He saw to it that the money was used for its true purpose, down to the last piece of copper.

Two skillful commoners, the brothers Gaspard, reorganized and increased the dauphin's artillery. Now there was money to pay the arrears due to the soldiers, and more money to pay for the equipment of a larger army.

At long last the dauphin could dare to move toward the ancient city where all French kings had been crowned. With him went the strongest army he ever had, commanded by the greatest names of France and . . . by the Maid.

Even so, the town of Auxerre, French since the year 1300, but Burgundian at heart, would not open its gates and acknowledge the dauphin to be its king. The town council sent a message that they would declare themselves for the dauphin only if, and when, the towns of Troyes, Chalons, and Rheims would do the same.

"Fine," La Hire jeered, "and if we have to fight these towns, the men from Auxerre will take us from the rear."

Joan pleaded for an immediate attack on the town, but this time the opinion of the cautious commanders prevailed. The army moved on, leaving Auxerre undefeated in the rear.

The good citizens of Troyes tried exactly the same recipe. After all, Auxerre had got away with it, so why should not they? Besides, there was a rumor that the Duke of Bedford was on the march.

The Duke de La Trémoïlle insisted on negotiations. They went on for five days and led nowhere. In the meantime, food became scarce. Finally the dauphin insisted on calling in the Maid.

"Give me full powers again, gentle dauphin," Joan said, "and the town will be yours. You will enter it tomorrow."

"I give you full powers", the dauphin said quickly, before anybody could speak against it.

The Maid left and at once gave the orders for a general alarm.

The citizens heard the noise. They manned the walls and saw the entire French army getting ready for an assault. Good heavens, they had not bargained for *that* sort of thing! The Bishop of Troyes declared in favor of the dauphin and the Maid. There followed a violent quarrel between the citizens and the Burgundian garrison.

Night fell, the worst night Troyes had known for many years. Tomorrow perhaps not one house would remain standing. The French had deployed their artillery. The women pleaded with their men to open the gates.

In the morning the French trumpeters gave the signal for a general attack. The troops began to move.

Before the first shot was fired, the gates opened and the municipal authorities came out. They had taken the bishop with them to make sure that they would not be killed. Even so, they trembled as, kneeling before the dauphin and his commanders, they asked his pardon for having been so obstinate. But there was that Burgundian garrison who had practically forced them to resist, so what could they do . . . ?

The dauphin gave his pardon with a smile. As for the

Burgundian garrison, he would allow it to leave with all their arms and all their possessions.

The Burgundian garrison left, but, as they were marching past the French army, Joan saw that they were taking a number of French prisoners with them. "In the name of God," she cried, "that I will not allow to happen."

The Burgundians had the boldness to protest. The dauphin had given his word that they could take all their possessions with them, and these prisoners were part of their possessions.

For a few moments it looked as if there would be fighting after all.

The dauphin rode up. When he was told about the incident, he laughed. "I'll buy those men from you", he said. "Why wait for ransom if you can have it here and now?"

The Burgundians were delighted. So, unnecessary to say, were the French prisoners. Even the Maid smiled a little.

Most impressed of all, however, were the mayor and councillors of Troyes. What a statesmanlike solution! With a few hundred francs, the dauphin had bought himself a number of friends at the Burgundian court, as well as getting his prisoners back. There was something about that young prince after all. They decided to write to Rheims and to recommend to the authorities there to open their gates straight away. "We have all been misinformed about the dauphin . . ."

The dauphin turned to Joan. "Once again your advice was right," he said, "and you shall enter my good city of Troyes ahead of me—now!"

From Troyes the dauphin himself wrote a letter announcing his arrival to the city of Rheims. There was no answer.

The town of Chalons opened its gates at once and proclaimed itself for the dauphin and the Maid. A second letter went to Rheims, and after that a third. Still there was no answer.

There seemed to be something uncanny about this prolonged silence. A great deal of whispering was going on around the Duke de La Trémoïlle. Archbishop Regnault of Chartres also did not know what to make of it all, although Rheims was the seat of his own archdiocese.

The Maid insisted on action. The army was to march on, even quicker than before. Most of the artillery could not follow the pace, and now many of the military commanders began to become worried.

In Rheims the commanders of the garrison and the heads of the municipal council were having one conference after another. As long as the dauphin was having his little skirmishes far away in the Loire region, they had felt quite safe in being pro-Burgundian. But now the danger was creeping nearer and nearer. The dauphin wanted to be crowned here. That was something the

Duke of Burgundy and the English would never forgive Rheims for . . . if it ever took place.

A few months ago the whole thing looked like sheer lunacy. No one thought of taking it seriously for a moment. But now? There was a huge army marching toward Rheims, and with it that strange creature. One did not know whether she was a saint or a witch, but one decidedly did know that she was extremely dangerous unless one did exactly what she wanted.

Could the commanders hope to resist an attack of that army and of the terrible Maid successfully? Could they guarantee it?

Most embarrassing questions were asked in rapid succession and never quite satisfactorily answered. There was no guarantee in war. One would have to see what happened. Perhaps the French army was not quite as large as news would have it. Perhaps . . .

Bishop Pierre Cauchon, sharp-featured, gray-faced, spoke up for the Duke of Burgundy, to whom he owed his bishopric of Beauvais. It was idiotic to sacrifice the great duke's protection and favor for that of a prince who was known only for his weaknesses and who had been the laughingstock of the whole country until the services of a wild-eyed adventuress made him dangerous. "It won't be for long, you may rest assured of that. Adventurers and adventuresses never last long. We shall see this one go, too—all of us, even the oldest of us."

There was such deep hatred in the dark voice that the good councillors shuddered.

"Receive the dauphin," Bishop Cauchon went on, "crown him—and in one year, in a few months perhaps, and maybe still less, you will all lose your heads."

"But the people, the masses", the mayor dared to remind him. "So many of them are for that . . . that girl. They are pestering me at my office, at my home. They don't want to be besieged and to suffer instead of having the joy of a crowning ceremony—"

". . . and all the money that kind of thing invariably means for their pockets", Cauchon added drily. "But don't forget that the dauphin is a beggar. What little money they scraped together for him had to be spent on the army. The very first thing he is bound to do is to raise fresh taxes. The citizens will love the town councillors for it, will they not? Ah, well, I have no voice in your council, although Beauvais will fall if Rheims has fallen. But if I had, I would say: close your hearts to the dauphin's appeal; close your gates to him and his army; and close your ranks to resist him and his adventuress until the Duke of Bedford's army appears in their rear."

But the mayor was listening to the noise in the street. "Do you hear that, my lord bishop? They're clamoring for what they already call their king! How can I resist an army, and a large one at that, when I can no longer rely on the loyalty of the city? How can I know where my own loyalty ought to be . . . ?"

"Exactly", one of the councillors fell in, encouraged by the noise outside, despite Bishop Cauchon's dark looks. "You are a man of the Church, my lord bishop, and a learned man as well; you know that here in Rheims Saint Remigius crowned the first king of the Franks almost a thousand years ago."

"Every child knows that", snapped Cauchon.

"You think the Maid is an adventuress", the councillor went on. "Well, may be she is. But it's strange all the same that she should hail from the village of Domrémy in Lorraine, *Remigii domus*, the house of Remigius, named after that very saint . . ."

Cauchon snorted. "The air is full of pseudoprophecies and the predictions of fools, Messire councillor. What shall we come to if men in high positions such as yours will listen to that kind of thing?"

"If only the Duke of Bedford would come", the mayor groaned.

From afar came trumpet signals.

"What is that?" asked the bishop, frowning.

"I don't know", the mayor murmured. He looked a little pale. "It's the signal for good news, but how could that be? I wonder . . ."

Hasty steps were heard outside on the corridor. There was a slight knock, and the town clerk entered. "Sieur Mayor, Sieur Mayor, why didn't you tell me . . . ?"

"Tell you what?" the mayor asked.

"That you have given orders to have the gates opened, of course", the town clerk said, trembling with righteous indignation. "I should have been told. How can I get the keys ready, and the cushion and the insignia of the city?"

"What are you babbling, man?" the mayor barked. "Who said I gave orders to open the gates? And for whom?"

"For the dauphin, of course", the town clerk stammered. "His vanguard is coming in by the east gate. The militia commanders opened it for them. He'll be here in half an hour. And I'm in my everyday clothes—and so are you, Sieur Mayor . . ."

"The militia has gone over to the dauphin", the mayor stammered. "By the saints, by all the saints, what do we do now?"

"Go to the east gate, of course", said the councillor who had mentioned Saint Remigius and the village named after him. "We cannot let the dauphin be received merely by the militia and the rabble. The town must be represented worthily."

"You're right." The mayor rang the bell for his servants. "My hat, my stick, my chain", he ordered. "All the clerks will assemble in five minutes. We must go to the east gate." Suddenly he remembered the Bishop of Beauvais. "Well, my lord bishop," he said, "and what do you say now?" Smiling, he turned toward the bishop's chair. It was empty.

"His lordship left a minute ago", the town clerk said. "He seemed to be in a great hurry."

"And so would I be, if I had said what he said." The mayor put on the chain of office that a servant handed him on a red cushion. He clapped his hat on his bald pate and seized his stick with the golden knob. "Let us go", he said, "and render homage to the dauphin . . . to the king, I mean, of course."

"Vive le roi!" they cried in the streets of Rheims. "Long live the king!"

Flags and pennants, carpets and draperies were hanging out of the windows, and everybody was wearing Sunday dress. This was the day of days, the day of coronation, and for most of the citizens it was the first time that such a thing happened. It had been almost fifty years since the last coronation.

There had been precious little time for suitable preparations, and yet this coronation really needed more preparation than any other before. It seemed as if practically everything that was most urgently needed was missing, above all, the very insignia of royalty: the crown. The crown, the ancient crown of the French kings, could not be found. The mayor had all his officials search for it. He was frantic; what greater shame could there be for Rheims than to have mislaid the royal crown! Dozens of buildings were searched from cellar to roof; several altars in the cathedral were removed. In the end they found it under masses of discarded vestments in a sacristy. But the royal cloak was missing, too, and so was the ancient sword and, most important of all, the holy oil, the Sacred Ampoule with the coronation oil that, according to the legend, was first used by King Clovis of the Franks and always kept its level. They found it at the monastery of Saint Rémy, and the abbot himself took it to the cathedral for its solemn purpose.

Within a few hours all silk, brocade, and leather disappeared from the shops and warehouses. All the seamstresses of the city had to go on working throughout the night, for there was not a single lady who did not wish to wear a brand-new dress for such an occasion.

Strangers arrived from everywhere. Thousands of them had left their hometowns weeks before, as if they had known for certain that and when the great event would be taking place. All the inns and hostelries were crammed full with guests, and more were arriving by the hour.

The Maid, too, had no sleep the night before. She spent it praying right through. She did not think of tomorrow only; in fact, she scarcely thought of it at all. She had known for a long time that this would happen, that God had chosen her through his saints to bring it about. But after that, what was she to do? The English were still holding half of France. Surely God did not want her to do only half the work? Surely this was not to be the end of her mission?

Yet, however much she prayed, the Voices would not come, her dear, beloved Voices, so deeply disturbing at times, so sweetly reassuring at others. The Voices remained silent. . . .

They were still silent when the young day rose, the great day for Rheims and for France, the great day for the dauphin.

"Your great day has arrived", La Hire told her, when she stepped out into the street, where a glittering retinue of nobles was waiting for her. "Today all is coming true what you predicted. A proud day for you!"

"God forbid", she said, terrified. "God forbid that this day should make me proud." How often she had searched her conscience to see whether she was still the humble servant of the Lord and his saints, whether the constant admiration and adulation of the people, of great nobles, of the dauphin himself had not made her proud. She knew that in that case she would no longer be God's instrument as before. All that happened was God's work, and he alone should be given the honor for it. He had chosen her not because she merited to be chosen, but because it had pleased him to do so. She was his instrument, and he could drop her at any moment if it pleased him to do so. She was his creature; she belonged to him. He had made her, and all she had was his, not hers. If he chose to take it all away again, she had no right to complain.

They escorted her to the cathedral, through throngs of people, acclaiming her, praising her to the skies, calling her the liberator of France, the greatest woman France ever produced, a saint. They were trying to kiss her hand, her foot, the hem of her cloak.

"My Lord and my God," she prayed, "keep the sin of pride away from me."

Through wave after wave of thunderous applause she went on, until she reached the main door of the cathedral—that wonder of architecture, greater and more beautiful than Notre Dame, indeed than any other church in France, except only the cathedral of Chartres.

Here at the door she took her place with many of the nobles at the side of the entrance. Here also Archbishop Regnault de Chartres was waiting with a wreath of prelates in red, white, and purple around him, and with the Bishops of Laon, Chalons, Séez, and Orléans.

All the church bells of Rheims were ringing incessantly.

Heralded by fanfares of a hundred trumpets and by the roaring of the crowds, the dauphin appeared, dressed in cloth of gold and followed by hundreds of nobles. As he approached the cathedral door he saw the Maid.

"Joan," he said, "follow me and stand behind me with your banner when I am anointed, for such is your place by right on this day."

For a moment her thoughts were comforted by the happiness she saw in his face. She obeyed and followed him into the cathedral.

The young man with the homely face had to speak a solemn oath to maintain the peace and the privileges of the Church, to protect his people from unjust demands, and to rule with justice and mercy. Then the Duke of Alençon armed him as a knight. Two great nobles lifted him up together with his chair, while two others held the crown high above his head. Thus he was "shown to the people", as in times of old when a king was chosen by acclamation of the people and lifted up on his shield.

When he was put down again, the venerable old Abbot of Saint-Rémy anointed him with the holy oil.

"*Noël!*" shouted the multitude in the huge cathedral. The old French cry of joy rang out, for the happiness of seeing the coronation was to them equal to the joy of Christmas. "*Vive le roi! Noël!* Long live Charles the Seventh!"

The Maid knelt before him, and at once there was breathless silence.

"My noble king," she said in a trembling voice, "God's will has been fulfilled that I should raise the siege of Orléans and lead you to Rheims to be anointed. Now it is for all to see that you are the true and only king, chosen and entitled to the realm of France."

The king himself lifted her up. Once more the cathedral walls echoed the enthusiastic shouts of the glittering assembly. Few people saw that there were tears in the eyes of the Maid.

11

FRANCS FOR THE MAID

WEEKS AND WEEKS OF TALKING followed the great event of the coronation. The news spread everywhere. From all over France the keys of a great number of cities and towns were sent to the new king, as a sign of submission and loyalty. Hope was rising, in many cases wildly exaggerated, that there could be a new golden age under the rule of the young monarch, assisted by the Maid, a chosen instrument of God. Around the young monarch himself nothing much happened.

Both Burgundians and English remained sharply hostile. Paris was still in their hands, and the whole of Normandy. The peace party at the young king's court pleaded for a truce, for negotiations. For a while they prevailed, mainly perhaps because the Maid remained silent. She was still with the dauphin, but she did not press her counsel on the king as she had done on the dauphin.

Her Voices were silent. . . .

Only the army protested. The army had learned the taste of victory. "Wherever the Maid is fighting, there is victory", the soldiers said; "give us the Maid, and let's get on with the war.

"What shall I do, Joan?" the king asked her. He had to summon her to his presence; she no longer came uninvited.

"I don't know, Sire. I don't know."

Some of her enemies hoped she would try her hand again. "One defeat, and she ceases to be a danger."

Their chance came soon enough. Charles was the king, but he was a king without a capital. Paris, Paris must be reconquered. . . .

They sent La Hire to see the Maid—faithful, gruff La Hire, who did not believe in ruses and intrigues and who was only too glad to persuade Joan to new adventures. Surely her mission was not yet fulfilled—not completely—as long as the English were still on French soil, as long as the king could not set foot into his own capital? She and she alone could change all that. Was she going to shirk it? The army was calling for her!

She accepted. Her heart was heavy, but she accepted. Once she was again with the soldiers, all worry and anxiety subsided in her. This was her world; here were her friends. The political situation too seemed to point out that she was right. Negotiations with the Burgundians had broken down. The enemy had never taken them seriously, but regarded them only as a measure to gain time, to recover from the shock of their defeats and of the final shock of the coronation.

The first assault on Paris ended with a defeat. Fifteen hundred French soldiers lost their lives, the Maid herself was wounded twice, and the Duke of Alençon had to carry her back out of reach of the enemy fire. As soon as the Maid came to, on her field-bed, she ordered a second assault, but special envoys of the king arrived in camp, and the king's message was: the Duke of Alençon and the Maid were forbidden to repeat the assault on Paris.

Joan bit her lip. Her eye fell on her banner. The Duke of Alençon had saved it. Beside it was her armor, pierced in the two places where she had been wounded, and her sword. And the sword was broken. Her sword, the sacred sword from Fierbois, broken right at the hilt! Joan cried.

Trickery was in the air, trickery and deceit. Joan no longer knew on whom she could rely. She did not know how strong the position of her enemies had become at court, but she could see some of the consequences. The

Duke of Alençon left the army and returned to his young wife. Dunois was back in Orléans; La Hire was sent on bold little adventures far away. Her friends were eliminated cleverly, one by one.

Secret negotiations were going on again with the Duke of Burgundy. Joan herself desired nothing better than peace with that powerful leader, but she knew his true nature well enough to insist that he must first be overcome by force.

Bishop Cauchon had had to flee from his seat in Beauvais very shortly after the coronation. Now he was in Rouen and from there laid a careful web of intrigues. He had never believed in the mission of the Maid. His sympathies were entirely Burgundian. To him Joan was either a misguided girl posing as saint, or a witch. She had shed streams of blood. She had cost him his bishopric, at least for the time being. She must be defeated and caught at all costs.

By now the greater part of the French army was disbanded, although there was no peace, not even a truce. The Maid went on fighting with small bodies of men. She conquered Saint-Pierre-le-Moustier, but had to abandon the siege of La Charité-sur-Loire for lack of equipment.

Her base was now Compiègne, her force not much more than two thousand men. One night, at Melun, she felt that strange feeling that always preceded the hearing of her Voices. She fell on her knees, and the Voices came. "Joan, you will be taken prisoner before

Saint John's day. This must be. . . . Take all with a willing heart. God will help you."

She prayed to be allowed to die quickly and not to have to face a long ordeal.

The young commander of Compiègne had a short conference with Joan. "The town is in dire danger", he said. "The Burgundians are threatening us from one side and the Godons from the other. If we do not succeed in keeping at least a channel open so that we can get convoys of food in, we are lost. Therefore, everything depends upon one thing . . ."

"The bridgehead at Margny", Joan interposed, and the commander gave her a look of admiration. He had often wondered whether the famous Maid was really such a gifted tactician as some people seemed to believe. Now he knew that she was that—whatever else she might be.

"Yes, that bridgehead", he nodded. "Do you think you can get it?"

"Only in one way", Joan said thoughtfully. "By surprise."

She left Compiègne with d'Aulon and five hundred men. Over her armor she wore a coat of scarlet and gold. She wanted to make sure that her soldiers could always see her—and she loved vivid colors.

But the enemy saw her too. Jean de Luxembourg, a commander of the Burgundian forces, was out and about with a dozen nobles to get a clearer picture of the terrain around Compiègne. He saw her. Only just in time, he and his little group turned away and rode off as quickly as their horses would carry them. As soon as they were back, riders were sent speeding off to the English forces and to the Duke of Burgundy himself. "The Maid has come out of her lair", the message went. "If you are quick, we may catch her."

Then Jean de Luxembourg attacked. He was not out to win this fight, but only to hold this dangerous enemy, to keep her busy until the duke and the English arrived.

Joan too attacked, and the two forces met with a resounding crash. As so often before, the attack of the Maid proved irresistible. She drove Luxembourg's forces back and penetrated deeply into the village of Margny. But from the rear came the sound of trumpets, and Joan turned in the saddle and listened. The trumpets were not French. They were English. In the next moment d'Aulon rode up to her. "The Godons are coming", he reported breathlessly. "They're cutting off our retreat."

"Why retreat?" Joan cried. "Think only of attacking them."

But for the first time in her life she did not succeed in rallying her men. The fear of being taken between two enemy forces, perhaps also the very nearness of Compiègne and safety, made them run for their dear lives.

She did what a valiant commander must do in such circumstances. She fought desperately to shield her retreating force and give them time and breathing space to reach the saving fortress. D'Aulon, faithful to the last, kept at her side, warding off pike thrusts and the blows of maces and swords.

The scarlet coat attracted the enemy as a burning candle the moths. They were milling all around her, hacking their way toward her. A dozen hands tried to grasp her. An archer from Picardy seized her coat and pulled with all his might. She fell heavily.

"The Maid", shouted the archer. "I've got the Maid."

"Surrender", a Burgundian knight cried, as she struggled to her feet.

"I will not surrender to you", she said defiantly. "I have already surrendered to God, and to him I will keep my word."

But they seized her.

The Maid was a prisoner.

She was not treated too badly. The archer who pulled her off her horse was one of Jean de Luxembourg's men. Thus, by the rules of war she was Jean de Luxembourg's prisoner, although that worthy was himself a vassal of the Duke of Burgundy. He took her first to his head-quarters. There the Duke of Burgundy paid her a visit, curious to see the girl who had done so much harm to his cause and that of his English allies. She paid no attention to him.

Thoroughly annoyed, he went back to Coudun, where he dictated a triumphant letter to be sent to the citizens of Saint-Quentin, and copies of it to other towns. "I have not lost a single man in this battle. None of us was wounded, none killed, none taken prisoner. The enemy's losses were severe. It was the pleasure of God that the Maid should become a prisoner. This, assuredly, will be great news everywhere and expose the error and the madness of those who favored that woman."

"That woman" was now transported to the castle of Beaulieu-en-Vermandois. Soon that place, strong as it was, was regarded as still too exposed to guard so dangerous a prisoner. She was taken to the castle of Beaurevoir. For the time being, Jean de Luxembourg still behaved as befitted a nobleman. The prisoner was treated well and looked after by her captor's own wife, aunt, and stepdaughter.

Nevertheless, she suffered. She could no longer do anything for her beloved country. She was a prisoner. She dreaded that she might be delivered into the hands of the English. And Compiègne, entrusted to her by the king . . . What would become of Compiègne, now that she was no longer there to defend it?

She decided to escape, but Jean de Luxembourg had provided for such a plan. Heavily armed men guarded all the doors.

Desperate, she mounted the high tower of the castle and . . . jumped. It was a jump of more than sixty feet. Half an hour later they found her lying unconscious on the ground. When she came to, they accused her of having tried to commit suicide. She was indignant. "How could I do something so sinful? I was just trying to escape." In the end they believed her, but now they were more afraid of her than ever. How could she have survived such a jump?

That night Saint Catherine appeared to her and told her that she must ask God's pardon for her rash deed. She did—and the saint had a word of comfort for her, too: Compiègne would not fall to the enemy but would be relieved before Saint Martin's Day, November 11.

She told the news to everyone. In the first days of November it came true.

Her enemies had been busy too. In the same month Jean de Luxembourg was offered a substantial sum of money for the Maid—not by the king who owed his throne to her, not by the nobles whom she had led from victory to victory, but by the English.

His family pleaded with him; his old aunt even begged him on her knees not to dishonor himself and his good name. But he did not dare to incur the disfavor of the Duke of Burgundy and of his powerful English allies. Besides, six thousand francs was a very large sum. He sold the Maid.

Soon she was carried off again, first to Arras and then by stages to Rouen. Two great powers now took over: the English, and Pierre Cauchon, Bishop of Beauvais, who had fled from his bishopric to his English and Burgundian allies.

Here in Rouen she was to be tried. Far too intelligent to take the trial into their own hands, the English decided on an ecclesiastic court, presided over, of course, by the Bishop of Beauvais. Of his feeling toward Joan they were sure.

Very thorough preparations were made. They lasted for many months.

Meanwhile, Joan was given a cell in the ordinary prison. She was put in chains. Five soldiers had to guard her cell by day and night.

HONOR RESTORED

News of the trial was scanty in the parts of France not occupied by the English or by the Burgundians. It was known that both La Hire and Dunois tried to raid Rouen and to liberate her, but with sadly insufficient forces. Many people believed that the peace party around the king was powerful enough to see to it that such expeditions failed.

Certainly there were many important people at court who were glad to be rid of such an unpredictable girl.

Grown bold by her successes in the past, they said, she might plunge the country into a disastrous adventure. The worst hypocrites among them took the point of view: "If she is a saint, God will know how to help her in her plight; he does not need us for that. And if she is not, why help her?"

But many good bishops and priests were horrified about what they heard. Why, the whole trial could never even be valid! Bishop Cauchon had no jurisdiction outside of his diocese. He belonged to Beauvais, not to Rouen. Besides, she had been examined and interrogated very thoroughly before she had been given her first command. Archbishop Regnault de Chartres himself, although not exactly her warmest friend, had had to acknowledge that there was no wrong in her.

Surely, surely it would not come to the worst. They would not, they could not, condemn her to death. They might imprison her, and sooner or later one would be able to do something for her.

Some of her answers in court became known—lovely, spirited answers. Thus when one of the judges asked her: "Dare you say that you are in a state of grace?" she replied: "If I am not, may God bring me to it; if I am, may God keep me in it." No one would dare condemn a girl who gave such an answer.

Another thing she said was: "Before seven years have passed, the English will suffer a defeat much worse than they did at Orléans; they will lose a much greater prize. The king will be established in his kingdom whether his enemies wish it or not. . . . I know for a certainty that the English will be driven out of France—all, that is, except those who will die here."

So she was still making bold predictions! Bold indeed, for a girl in the hands of her enemies, chained, and delivered to their mercy. But then she always said exactly what she felt—or what her Voices told her. In France grave-faced men wagged their heads. A pity she could not bridle her tongue in such a situation. Of course, what she said might well be true. After all, everything she had said so far had come true. . . .

On the other hand, it was just that outspokenness, that way of saying things bluntly, whether one liked it or not, that had made her so many enemies at the king's court. . . .

There was a rumor that she had recanted. Promptly the very people who had hoped she would be more adaptable and diplomatic were alarmed. If she had re-canted—if she had admitted that she was not sent by God, that her Voices were not those of the archangel Michael and of the saints—by what power then had she raised the siege of Orléans and brought the king to Rheims to be crowned? To whom, in such circum-stances, did the king owe his crown?

Yet, at that very moment, Joan in court defended her king in words stronger than those she used in her own defense: "I tell you, sir, with all respect, and I will swear to it and risk my life on it, that this king whom you outrage with your words is the noblest Christian of all

Christians, that no one bears a greater love to the
Church, and that he is not what you say he is!"

She was shouted down.

When Durand Laxart entered the house of the d'Arcs,
all faces lit up for a moment. Jacques d'Arc shook his
hand. So did his son, and even Isabelle Romée gave him
a smile, but it froze on her lips when she saw the expression on his face. Durand Laxart looked weary and sad, he
had aged, his hair was graying all over; his eyes were
shifty and gleaming strangely. If ever a man looked like
the harbinger of bad news . . .

"Where are you coming from?" Jacques d'Arc asked.
"We haven't seen you for almost a year."

"I am coming from Rouen", Durand answered
slowly.

"From . . . from the trial?" asked Isabelle, trembling.

"The trial is all over", Durand replied gravely. "Jacques,
Isabelle, Jean . . . I have . . . very terrible news . . ." His
voice failed him.

"Is Joan alive?" Isabelle asked, and God alone knew
what strength she needed to ask it.

Durand Laxart shook his head. Tears were trickling
down his face. Isabelle fell into her chair. Jacques d'Arc
bit his lip, hard. His son cried out: "What have they
done to her?"

Durand crossed himself. He took a deep breath.
"Burned her", he gasped. "Burned her. As a witch and a
heretic. On the marketplace. Our Joan."

Jacques d'Arc gave a sobbing cry and ran out of the room.

Jean raised his fists. "Cousin Durand," he screamed, "where is God? Where is God that such a thing could happen?"

"*Credo*", came an almost toneless voice. "I believe in God, the Almighty Father, Creator of Heaven and earth. . . ." Isabelle Romée went on and on. Her face was like snow.

Later that day Durand Laxart had to tell everything he knew. "The English wanted her dead", he said. "She was too dangerous an enemy for them, even as a prisoner. That word of hers that the English would all be driven out of France went around very quickly. And Bishop Cauchon wanted her dead, too. He wanted the glory of having rid the English and the Burgundians of their great enemy. They say he wants to be Archbishop of Rouen. He and his clique did everything to bring about her condemnation."

"The Church has condemned my daughter as a witch and a heretic", Jacques d'Arc groaned. "The Church— my own Church . . ."

"No", said Isabelle Romée strongly.

The men looked at her.

"Not the Church", Isabelle said. "Only a few bad servants of the Church; and God will take care of them."

"You're right", Durand said eagerly. "I have proof for that, Jacques. She is right. They had such a large assembly of theologians together, Dominican friars too. But one after the other dropped out. Some Bishop Cauchon got rid of, as soon as he saw that they were for her—like Father Lohier, one of the most learned of them all, who said it was all invalid. All the Dominicans were for her, oh, so many of them, except the Inquisitor, and he was such a weak man. He never dared to stand up against Bishop Cauchon, and they say that is why the bishop chose him.

"The good Fathers de la Pierre and Ladvenu tried to save her more than once, and so did Fathers Delachambre and Tiphaine and Gronchet and Minier and Pigache and others. The learned Licentiate La Fontaine was for her. I can't remember them all, there were so many. The English Lord Warrick or Warwick threatened the priests for helping her, and then the bishop decided upon excluding the public. We could only hear rumors for a while. Rouen was talking of nothing else. Oh, the answers Joan gave them! How stupid some of the learned men looked when she spoke! And when they asked questions that were so wrong even a simple man like me could see it, she just said, 'Next question.'"

"It was an unjust thing", Isabelle said. "The Holy Father must know about it. The king must know about it."

"There has never been a more unjust thing", Durand cried, "since our blessed Lord was condemned by Annas and Caiphas."

Isabelle Romée could not smile. No one ever saw her

smile again since that day. But she gave him a grateful look.

"The prosecutor they appointed was Estivet," Durand went on, "a man of Beauvais, full of hatred because he had to flee with his bishop when the king came into his own. They threatened her and threatened her and hounded her with questions, day after day, week after week, for months on end. Once, and once only, she broke down. By Almighty God, I who am a man and not a girl, I would have broken down a hundred times. She just could go on no longer, and she said she must have been mistaken after all. All Rouen knew soon enough that Cauchon and Estivet and the English were furious, because now that she had recanted they could not condemn her to death. So they tricked her, tricked her into what they called a relapse, but by then Joan had recovered her strength. She spoke up again as boldly as ever and so well that an English noble who was present said: 'This is a good girl, to be sure; what a pity she is not English!' Her Voices had spoken to her again, and she told the court that they had said to her: 'Take all with cheerfulness. Do not shrink from your martyrdom for through it you will come to paradise.'"

"She is in Heaven", said Isabelle Romée stonily. "My daughter is in Heaven. No one can tell me that she is not."

"They were furious about her calling herself a martyr," Durand continued, "for how could the Church condemn anybody to martyrdom, they said. One of the good fathers told me: 'It is all the most terrible injustice, and Bishop Cauchon knows it, for he has given her permission to receive Holy Communion. How could he do such a thing, if she were as he says she is, a heretic and renegade and a witch to boot? He did not dare to refuse it, but by granting her Holy Communion he has given proof that he does not think that she is what he says she is. Out of his own mouth he stands condemned.' I have learned his words by heart because I thought it would give you comfort when I could tell you about it."

"It was an unjust thing", Isabelle repeated with an almost unnatural calmness. "The Holy Father must hear about it. The king must hear about it."

She was a tower of strength, but even she broke down when Durand, because she insisted, told her about the end.

"When she was condemned to the death by fire, she said, 'Before God, the great Judge, I make complaint of the monstrous wrongs committed upon me.' Cauchon heard her say it, and he trembled. Instead of a judge she had made him an accused, and he felt it." Durand Laxart became more and more eloquent. He talked and looked like a man quite different from the simple farmer he used to be. It was as if the tragedy he had witnessed had made him grow.

"She had given the entire court fair warning", he went on. "She said: 'Take good care of yourselves, take good care, you who set yourselves up to be my judges, for you are taking a terrible burden on to yourself. Think well what you are doing, for I tell you truly that I was sent from God, and that you are putting yourselves in great danger. . . . I give you this warning, so that if our Lord punishes you, I shall have done my duty. . . .' and she cried aloud: 'I have come from God and my place is not here. Remit me into the hands of God, from whom I came.' But they would not, and they condemned her. She said to Cauchon: 'Bishop, it is because of you that I die.' He could not stand the way she looked at him when she said it. When she added: 'It is for your action in all this that I now summon you to stand before the bar of heaven', he left her cell in a hurry. It was then that he gave order that she should be allowed to partake of Holy Communion. He was worried about his own soul, as well he might be. Then they came and led her away. . . ."

"Go on", said Isabelle Romée. "Go on. Go on."

"They were in great haste to finish it", Durand said, and he grit his teeth. "They even forgot to give her a cross. It was an English archer, God bless him, who broke off two little branches from the kindling and tied them together with twine in the shape of a cross. She kissed it and took it with her. Then she spoke up and forgave all that had done her wrong and asked pardon of all whom she might have wronged herself in all her life. There was a good monk who tried to comfort her, and she asked him to step back, lest he be hurt by the flames . . ."

Jacques d'Arc beat his breast, sobbing. "My child, my child . . . "

"Go on", said Isabelle Romée.

"When the stake began to burn, she called upon our Lord and Saint Catherine and Saint Margaret and Saint Michael and again our Lord . . ." Durand Laxart's voice was cracking under the strain. "The name of Jesus was the last word she uttered." He took a deep breath. "There was much rabble on the place, and they shouted at her and some even laughed, but no one was shouting or laughing now. Many were in tears. All the priests present were in tears and looked very frightened, too. Not far away from where I stood, an English lord said something in a loud voice, and Friar Ladvenu, who can speak English, told me that he said: 'We are lost; we have burnt a saint.' Oh, Mother Isabelle, Mother Isabelle, I knew you wouldn't be able to stand it, but you did ask me to go on and on. . . ."

Isabelle Romée's head had sunk on her chest, and her thin arms were shielding her eyes. She was trembling all over. "Now they'll point at us with their fingers", Jacques d'Arc said bitterly. "Our daughter has saved France and crowned the king, but they'll point at us with their fingers."

"It doesn't matter what they do," said Jean, "but I wish I were dead."

Isabelle Romée withdrew her hands from her eyes. She looked up.

"I'm glad I am still alive", she said. "Somebody must be alive and act. . . ."

"What can we do?" Father d'Arc shrugged his weary

shoulders. "We're simple people. No one will listen to us. We can do nothing."

"Do nothing, then", Isabelle Romée replied. "I vow I will not rest until my daughter Joan's holy honor is restored."

Durand Laxart stared at her, bewildered. Her voice had sounded like Joan's, and she looked as if she were holding up a banner.

The Englishman who had cried out "we are lost; we have burnt a saint" was John Tressart, secretary to the King of England himself. He was not the only one who felt that way. One English soldier swore he had seen a white dove flying out of the flames. Another said he had seen the name of Jesus written in leaping flames.

One of the learned canons, Jean de Alespée, said openly, "May my soul one day be where I believe this girl's soul is now."

The master executor of Rouen went to see the Dominican friars the same evening, shaking with fright. "I have burnt a saint. God will never forgive me for it."

But all this was only the beginning.

Bishop Cauchon never became an archbishop. He died soon afterward, and so suddenly that he could not receive the sacraments. So did one of Joan's worst enemies during the trial, Loyseleur. Another, the Abbot of Jumièges, died only one month after Joan. The survivors began to be ridden with fear. One of the judges contracted the most terrible disease of the time, leprosy. The Duke of Bedford himself survived Joan by four years, but, when he died, he was defeated and near despair, a broken man. His end took place in the very castle where Joan had been a prisoner.

At that time the Burgundians at long last fell away from their English allies and formed a new alliance—with France. Five years after Joan's death the city of Paris opened its gates to the king, and Joan's prophecy was fulfilled that the English would lose a greater prize than Orléans before seven years were out.

On the king's desk was a petition on the part of Isabelle Romée to reopen the case of her daughter Joan, but he bided his time. He knew that before he could do so, he would have to get the documents of the trial of Rouen, still in English hands.

In the meantime Estivet, Joan's horrible prosecutor, died, and so did the Inquisitor Lemaistre.

Jacques d'Arc died of a broken heart and, soon after him, Joan's brother Jean. But Isabelle, not content with having sent her petition to the king, went off once more to Rome, despite her age, despite her frailty, to submit another petition to the Pope. She would not entrust anyone else with that mission. She went herself and in the same way as the first time—on foot.

In the meantime Rouen was conquered by the French and with it all the documentary evidence of the infamous trial. Now the king promptly acted. He issued "letters patent" to his counsellor, Doctor of Theology Guillaume Bouillé, declaring that Joan had been "killed unjustly, against reason and most cruelly", that he wished to find out the whole truth about the trial and the way it had been conducted, and that therefore all facts must be examined.

Soon the investigating theologians declared formally that the trial had been invalid and based upon evil assumptions instead of on facts. That was good enough for the king to know that he had a "good case". He also submitted the matter to the Pope.

Pope Calixtus III had only just ascended the throne. Submerged in work as he was, he still found time for old Isabelle Romée and her cause. What is more, he found it at once. Within two months from his coronation, he gave permission to start an ecclesiastic investigation and ordered the Archbishop of Rheims and the Bishops of Paris and of Coutance to go ahead with the matter straight away.

It was a thunderbolt, and its effect could be felt not only in France but in all Europe and, most strongly, of course, in England. It was not enough that the English had been beaten and hounded out of France—old Talbot, eighty years of age, had lost his life at Castillon in what was practically the last fight between French and English troops on French soil and the end of the Hundred Years' War; now it looked as if the "witch" burned at Rouen was coming to life again. It was a stain on the fair shield of England.

On November 17, 1455, the indomitable Isabelle Romée, now in her seventies, entered the cathedral of Notre Dame in Paris for a solemn ceremony. She was still dressed in mourning clothes and accompanied by her legal adviser, Father Maugier. The whole of Paris knew about it, and the huge cathedral was crammed full with people. They all rose as she entered as if she were royalty, and hundreds called out to her: "Good luck", "We are praying for you", and even "Pray for us, mother of a saint."

Looking neither right nor left, she walked up to the great assembly of ecclesiastics, prelates as well as learned doctors and professors of theology and of the law. Only when stating her case once more, the case for which she had fought so hard for so many years, her voice broke and she cried. Most of the spectators as well as of the clergy cried with her. After her, her legal adviser spoke too, demanding with great eloquence the official re-opening of the case of Joan of Arc.

Rarely in the history of the law was there a case so thoroughly gone into. Investigations took place independently in Rouen, Domrémy, Orléans, and Paris. Almost fifteen hundred witnesses gave their evidence.

On July 7, 1456, the final judgment was due.

Isabelle Romée was waiting patiently in the house of Father Mangier. She had no doubts about the outcome. She knew her daughter, and she believed in the justice of God and God's Church.

A multitude of people came streaming along the street,

with Father Mangier half-walking, half-carried in their midst.

Isabelle heard the noise outside, but she did not stir. Only when Father Mangier came in, beaming all over his round face, did she rise courteously. "Victory", he said breathlessly. "Victory, full and complete. The sentence of the trial of Rouen is quashed, nullified, void. A copy of it was solemnly torn to pieces in court."

"God is just", said Isabelle Romée.

"You should have heard the language the judges used", Father Maugier went on. "They said the sentence was contaminated with fraud, calumny, wickedness, contradictions, and manifest errors of fact and law. Today, those false judges of Rouen were on trial themselves, and their condemnation is final. It has been the Holy Father's explicit order that there should be no appeal from the judgment given today. Joan's innocence and their guilt will stand for all to see until the very end of time."

Isabelle Romée crossed herself. "It is well", she said quietly. "Now I can die in peace."

Isabelle Romée died two years later, in Orléans, the city of her daughter's great triumph, honored and loved by everybody.

Joan was never forgotten, but for several centuries her memory seemed to sleep in the hearts and minds of most people until, in 1909, a saint on the papal throne, Pope Saint Pius X, declared her blessed. In 1920, on May 9, Pope Benedict XV declared her a saint.

Tens of thousands, hundreds of thousands of French soldiers invoked her in battle during the terrible times of the First World War, 1914–1918. The great commander-in-chief of all the Allied troops in the last years of that war, Marshal Foch, never tired of pointing out that "the Maid" had been a brilliant strategist and tactician. French officers to this very day are learning from her!

In 1931, when the five-hundredth anniversary of her death was celebrated, the English Cardinal Bourne, Archbishop of Westminster, praised the saint who had fought so valiantly against his country, recalling that she had never hated her enemies, but wished them well. He quoted Joan's own words to the "Godons": "Go back to your homes, and God bless you."

In one of his books, a great British leader of the Second World War, Sir Winston Churchill, praised her at length.

In 1956 the five-hundredth anniversary of her rehabilitation was celebrated in Rouen, in the presence of the President of the French Republic. The beautiful cathedral, which had suffered so badly under the bombardment in the Second World War, was rebuilt. English Catholics, making reparation for the wrong the saint suffered in the long gone past, donated a special window.

The history of a saint continues to inspire, thanks first and foremost to the Church, who invokes her saints every day. As long as there will be men and women who love their country well enough to fight for its freedom, the memory of Saint Joan of Arc, the saint of soldiers, will never die.